Volume 1

"It Seems Like I've Been Here Before"

Steve Domanski
Scott Fabianek
Andrew French

This is a work of fiction.
All characters, events, and locations portrayed within are fictitious.

CIRCLES: VOLUME 1: IT SEEMS LIKE I'VE BEEN HERE BEFORE

Published by Fenris Publishing
Flagstaff, Arizona
https://www.fenrispublishing.com

ISBN 978-0-9719886-1-3

Printed in the United States, United Kingdom, or Australia
First printing July 2005
Second Printing June 2023

Cover and interior art by Scott Fabianek

Introduction and Exposition

Welcome, reader, to Circles. As I sit here, literally the night before the publication you hold in your hands is to be wisked to Canada for printing, I am struggling for something to say about the last six years of publishing Circles that has not already been said before. The years have been a rollercoaster of emotion, from the saddest events to the happiest days of my life. Rather than bore you with rehashing old tales, I find that I must simply recap the birth of Circles to you instead, as I hopefully remember it in my gaining years.

Yes, it is true, the commitment I made to the comic book did in fact start with the sentence, "If it doesn't suck, I'll publish it." (It has been my desire for many years to use that as our store's tagline: Comics That Don't Suck. But, I digress.) I do not remember the specific restaurant in which the final details were nailed down, but I do know that they had chicken wings on special that day, and the restaurant was near Scott's old apartment in Jamaica Plain. I have a theory that New England has the joyous charm of being what I like to call the "Triangle of Culinary Delight" formed by a general polygon of New England Culinary Institute, Culinary Institute of America in New York, and Johnson and Wales University in Rhode Island. This overabundance of good food must inspire the other artists as most of our good comic ideas tend to come in restaurants or over a meal. I tip my hat to the chefs.

Issue 0 was our test comic, six pages of "can we actually pull this off" to be published in our old paper catalog. (The story of the catalog, its untimely demise, and the company name change to follow is one for another time, hopefully involving heavy drink purchased on someone else's dime.) At the time, however, the teaser was a great way to kick start the comic, coming strong off the end of Lance Rund and Chris McKinley's Associated Student Bodies. Demand for gay furry comics was high, and with nothing filling its place, we knew we had a market and a fan base demanding more. We did not think of ourselves as being the replacement for ASB as much as another story to appeal to the same fans.

Little did I know the rabid following that Issue #1 would produce. And, little did I know that Scott would soon move off to California to live his dream of becoming an animator and working for the video game industry. The world never stands still. I moved to Waltham, Steve and Andy moved to Boston, and my loving boyfriend moved in with me. I switched jobs six times in that period of time, Steve twice and went back to school. And then my loving boyfriend became my loving husband. And then Steve and Andy got married, and Mike and Erich got married, and.... How we all had time to put out comic books with this craziness going on is beyond me. I applaud our fans for living with our mantra of "It's done when it's done."

I have a lot of people to thank for getting this book and the entire Circles series out the door. First, to my husband Andrew, he is the man who not only kept me sane throughout the years, but he did all the layout of this book. His contribution to this publication, the store, and my entire life could not be written in one simple introduction. All I can say is thank you for being the cutest fox in all the world.

Next, thank you to Lance Rund and Chris McKinley. Your work blazed the path for this comic. But, neither of us could have gotten this far without Howard Cruse. To him, we owe both the thanks that we may stand upon his shoulders as well as giving us the ability to reprint his very early work in issue #2. To all the cover artists, Chris Goodwin, T,' Margaret Petrie, thank you for your beautiful interpretations of the characters and your ability to get work in on time. To Mike and Carol Curtis, thank you for letting us latch on to your publishing house to get Circles into mainstream comic shops.

And, of course, I must thank Andrew French, Steve Domanski, and the illustrious Scott Fabianek for letting me share their work with you the public. I have said before that I have the artistic talent of a damp squid, so it is with humble thanks that I get to latch onto their talent and ride along the coat tales of mild fame.

Finally, to Harry, wherever you are.... Maybe we'll get that kiss next year.

To you, the reader, I thank you for your time and your enthusiasm. We look forward to serving you with the remainder of our tale in the years to come.

Sincerely,
Sean Rabbitt
Chief Bunny and Editor-In-Chief, Rabbit Valley® Comics

Circles
Created by:
Andrew French
Scott Fabianek
Steven Domanski
CircleS
ø
So, whaddaya think?
Well, um... It's very nice dear.... But, well, we don't look like that, and this never happens in the comic...
Ssssh! We'll sell more copies this way!

6 Kinsey Circle

Circles Issue 0

Introduction by Andrew French

This short strip originally appeared in a mail-order catalog that we gave away for free to advertise the book. Scott inked Marty by hand as black with white lines, and that got swallowed up in the printing process. Although it's still early, you can see some hints of where it's going. The relationship between Paulie, John, and Arthur is alluded to, as are Arthur's artistic talents. And the book Paulie buys is a book about living with AIDS, but his fingers cover most of the title, as we didn't want to give it away. We also displayed some of Doug's playful nature, Ken's overtly sexual nature and competitiveness, and, of course, a quick introduction of Marty. Actually, I'm pretty pleased with how much character development we packed into 4 pages.

Of special amusement is the detail of the calendar. I just told Scott I wanted a hot males calendar, and that's what he gave us. Thanks, Scott.

Damn! It's cold out there.
Hey, you live in Boston. Either get used to the cold or suffer in silence.

Oh, it's not so bad, Ken dear. I remember visiting my uncle in Edinburgh one Christmas holiday. That was cold!
Well, this is cold enough for me, thanks. Ooooh, he's cute!

Now now, children. We have serious business. We did not come just to shop.
Where? Lemme see.

Oh, hey. I didn't know Dan Savage was putting out a book...
Two years ago. Earth to Paulie.

Hey guys! Haven't seen you for a while.
Hello John!
Yo Johnny.

Jonathan, dear, how are you?
Oh, can't complain. You guys need help with anything?
Yes, thank you, John. May we post this on your bulletin board?
SHARE

Sure thing, Paulie. What's up?
Apartment for rent. Roger moved out, and Taye wants to find someone to split the rent with.
SHARE

Ooooh! Taye, huh? Mmm... I'd consider it. He's one sexy guy.
Frankly, I'd be glad to lower his rent. It's like taking money from family...

Paulie, we all talked about this. Taye doesn't want you to lower his rent. He can affford it fine. He just wants to share rent so he can put a few dollars away.
Doug, you must know by now that Paulie adopts everyone he knows. It's the reason we all love him, right?
Mmm, that's *one* of the reasons.

Want to know one of the other reasons, lover?
You can show me when we get home, you naughty thing.

What happened to the old days, Paulie? Remember when we used to go dancing? You, me, Arthur... How is Arthur anyhow?
He's fine. He asked me to say 'Hi.' Thanks for reminding me.
Living Wi
DAN S

Tell him 'Hi' back. He still painting? I was thinking of asking him to do some kind of mural on that blank wall outside.
Yes, he still paints quite a bit. I'll tell him you want to speak to him about it.

Besides, I appear to have traded youth for domestic bliss, and I have no complaints for the trade off.

These for me, Johnny.

If you miss the clubs, head down to Club Beat on Sunday. A bunch of us are going. Me, Taye...

Twenty years ago, I would have said yes without a pause. But, I think I'll pass. Thanks.

Suit yourself.

MEN OF
FIRE
FEBRUARY
APPARTMENT TO SHARE!!!

MEN OF
FIRE
MARCH
APPARTMENT TO SHARE!!!

MEN OF
FIRE
APRIL
Apartment to share, huh? Hmmmm...

I know the folks that are renting that place. Really nice. Some of my favorite customers.

Yeah, but this is dated January. They must've rented it out by now.
Never hurts to ask.

Hello? May I speak to Mr. Mayhew, please? Mr. Mayhew?
My name is Martin Miller. I'm calling about the ad you put up in Triangle Books?

Do you still have that apartment for rent?
RABBIT VALLEY
circles
TRIANGLE BOOKS

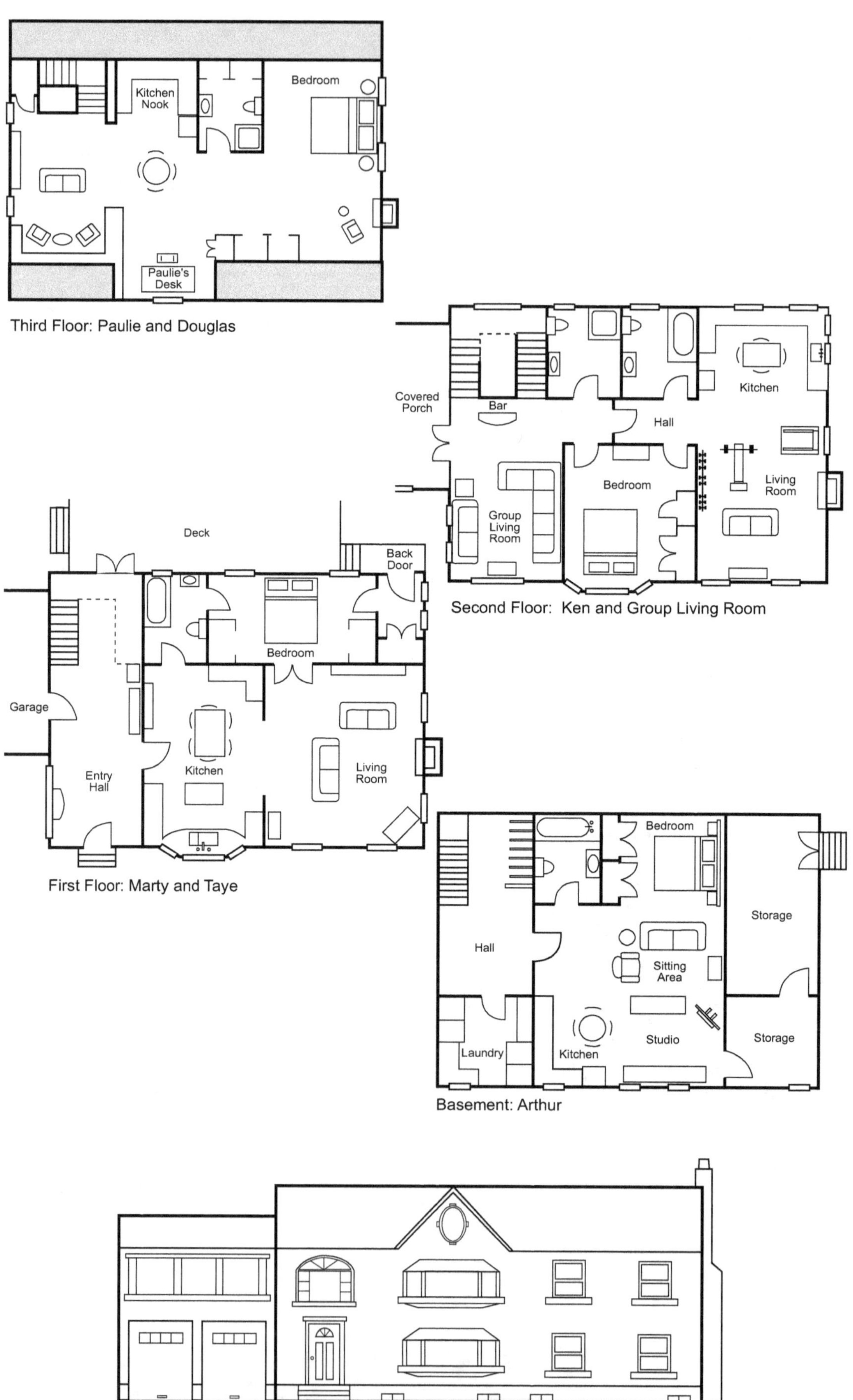

Third Floor: Paulie and Douglas

Second Floor: Ken and Group Living Room

First Floor: Marty and Taye

Basement: Arthur

$5.00
issue 1

6

Kinsey Circle

Circles Issue 1

Introduction by Andrew French

Issue One is set in mid-Spring of 2001, around Mother's Day. The title is from the Harry Chapin song "Circle," which also, incidentally, is where the whole book's title is from.

This is the comic that we really had to go back and revamp to bring it in line with the rest of the issues. An error in the printing led to Scott's pencil lines being visible, which a lot of people actually liked. It also led to the book being very dark. And don't even get me started about the fonts and font sizes we used. Oy.

You'll also note that some of the background details are missing. These were drawn by Steve when we realized how empty some parts of the book looked. The only ones we've chosen to replace are the tile wall and water effects in the shower scene. All the other ones we've omitted, both to make room for text and to just let Scott's work show off on its own.

And speaking of text... yes, I had to significantly edit the script for the comic to make it fit in a legible font size. This was a very painful process, but I think I tightened up the language while maintaining the important details. I am planning on posting the original script to the Yahoo Group we maintain, so, if you have never read Issue 1 and you want to see the entire original text, or if you just want to see what one of my scripts looks like, check it out.

And just as a random aside, the first panel of Taye (whom we'd kept hidden since the series was announced) was based on the first appearance of Mary Jane Watson in the Spider-Man comic. If the line "Face it, Tiger, you just hit the jackpot," means anything to you, you'll understand.

The
BOSTON SPHERE
Yet Another Mars Probe Goes Up Into Space
Flooding Continues Throughout Massachusetts
Dr. Laura TV Show is no more

How does one start writing?
Dear Diary
Journal 5 2001
Call me Ishmale
Oh, Hell...
What nonsense.
How does one start...

Dear Douglas...
Circles
Issue One: All My Life's a Circle

If I were blind, I would still know it was Spring. The smell of lilacs tells it it's nearly Mother's Day.
The smell of baking bread tells me Arthur's awake...
Unlike you, my sleepy-headed love.

I hear the Nussbaum grandkids playing, and I can just make out the riotous yellow of Kathy's forsythia bush.
Everywhere, the world is green, and the signs of Spring call out their yearly song...

"Come and dance with me..."

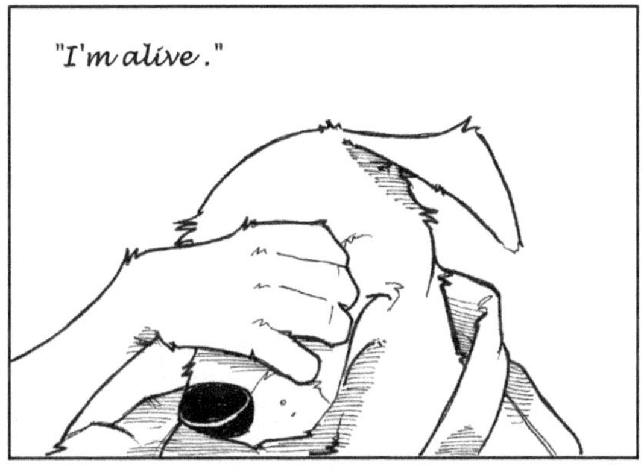
"I'm alive."

I'm sorry. I don't mean to get maudlin. I'll try to stick to what's actually happening.
As hard as that can be for a long-winded wanna-be poet.

Morning, love!
ungh

No morning kiss?

smek

Well, you just walked by, en route to the shower, I presume.
Hmm...shower. Not a bad idea.

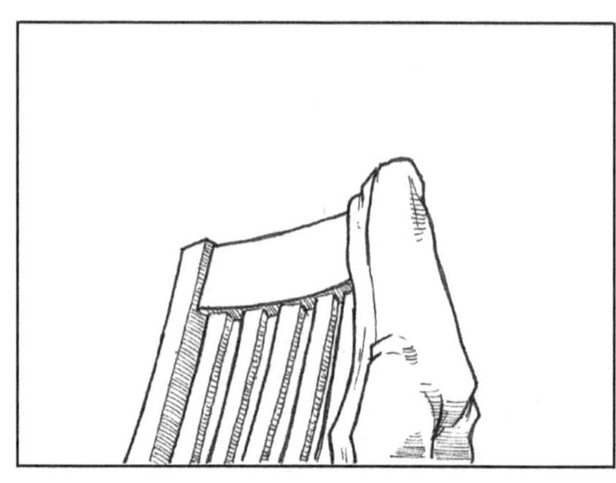

Why, hello there.
Hey, now. No funny stuff. I haven't had my coffee yet.

Ah, ha! That gives me the advantage.
Tsk! Molesting your half-conscious lover? Have you no shame?
I am pleased to report that I have none whatsoever

Alas, whatever shall become of me?
So what does today hold in the life of the idle rich?

Not so idle today. in fact. I'm seeing a prospective tenant.
To share with Taye? Who is he? Is he gay? Is he cute?
One at a time, dear. Yes, to share with Taye, if they get on. His name is Martin Miller, and he's a student at B.U. I haven't met him, so I don't know if he's cute.
As we posted the sign at Triangle Books, I think we can assume he's either gay, or *very* open-minded. I liked his voice on the phone. I have a good feeling about him.

You have good feelings about everyone.
That's not true! I have bad feelings about some people.
Name three.
Hitler. I have very bad feelings about Hitler.
Historical people don't count.

That's not fair. I was also going to say Anita Bryant and Regis Philbin.
Don't count.
Well, who do you have bad feelings for?

What?
Nothing.

Tell me.
Please.

I have bad feelings about the guy who got you sick.

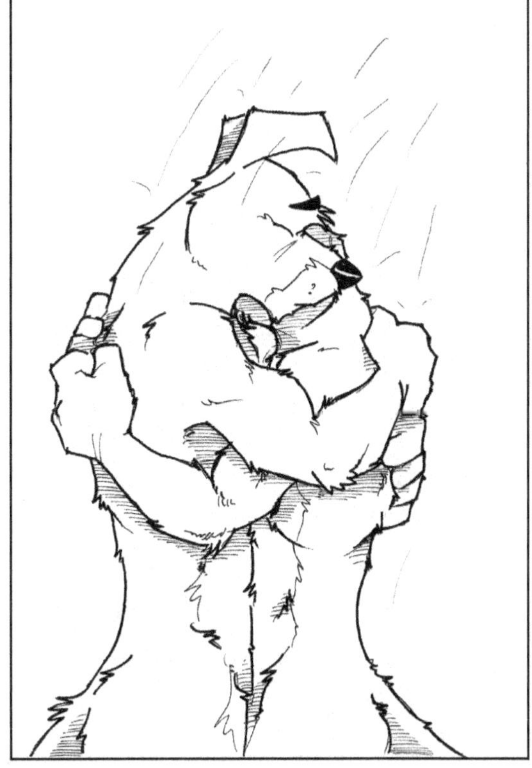

I'm sorry, Paulie. I don't mean to bring it up all the time. It just kind of slipped out.
It's okay, love. Really. Don't feel so bad.

Does it bother you a lot?
Not all the time. Some days go by, and I don't even spare it a single thought. Other days, it's all I *can* think of.

What about you?

I won't lie. It scares me.

We can talk about it anytime, love. This is something I'll always have to live with.
I don't want it to be this looming specter between us.

Okay. And the same goes for you, y'know.
I'm always here to talk to.

I know, love. Thank you.

What time will you be home?
About 3, but I have a Neighborhood Watch meeting at Mrs. N's house.
Ah, the esteemed Mrs. Nussbaum. Ask her how that fudge recipe worked out.

But will you be back in-between? I'll want your opinion of our prospective new tenant.
Yes. I'll need to change out of my "corporate back-stabber" costume.

You should wear a cuter tie, with baby ducks on it, or some such.
Baby ducks don't exactly say "ruthless, cold-hearted, financial genius", now do they?

Exactly! Think of how it would throw the others off.
They'll be wondering what you're up to.

Hmmm. It's a thought.
Oh, keep out of the plate of brownies, okay? Those are for the Watch.
I made you up a smaller plate to share with your guest, if you want.

By day, he destroys the weak. By night, he bakes brownies.

Yup. That's me.
Bye, love.
smek

8:30

Hmmm...

Uh, scuse me?

Oh, hello there! I'm afraid Ken's away at work.
Huh? Who's Ken?

Well, that's the door to Ken's place.
Um...this is 6 Kinsey Circle, isn't it?
Well, yes, but... Oh! Are you Martin Miller?

Uh, yes. Are you Mr. Mayhew?
My father is Mr. Mayhew. I'm Paulie.
Cool. Well, then, just call me Marty.

Well, Marty, could you help me out here? I'm running short of time, and I need to clean up here.
Oh, okay. I'll clean the clippers?
Excellent choice. I'll dispose of the weeds.

Well, why don't we head inside. It may only be spring, but it's plenty warm, and I know I could do with a drink. You?
Well, I'd like to see the place, of course, and...uh...a drink would be great.

Great place you have here, Mr. Mayhew.
Why thank you, Marty. And please, call me Paulie

Please. Sit. Relax. Iced tea okay?
Sure. Thanks.
Where are you from originally, Marty?

My family's from Maine, moved here a few years back. And you sound...
British?
Bravo. I was born in England, but my mother was American. I've lived here for years. Even majored in writing at Boston University.

Really? That's where I'm going!
I'm taking some business classes while I figure out my major.
Your tone suggests that business is not your passion?

Well, what I'd really like to get into is game design, like for computer games? I do pretty good work on a computer.
Well, if you do move in, I'd love to see one of your games. I was a fan of the early arcade classics.

Sure. I'd love to show 'em off. I haven't made many friends around here yet.
Well, we shall see what the future holds.
Now, let's get you a look at the apartment, hmm?

So, you'd be sharing the aprtment with Taye. I'm sure you'll get along famously. He works odd hours, but I believe he's just working a lunch shift today, so you'll be able to meet him soon.
What does he do?
Well, he's an actor by trade. He understudied Angel in Rent when it came through town last year.

Oh, yeah? I've heard of that.
Right now, he's between roles, so he's working at La Maison du Chanteur, that French restaurant where everyone sings. He's a very good singer, and quite a dancer, too.

And, here's the light switch...
Oh! Wow!

Seriously, wow! This kitchen is gigantic! The one at my folks' place is teeny compared to this.

Do you like to cook, dear?
Yeah. My Mom was really sick for a while when I was a teenager, so I learned to cook to avoid having to eat Mac n' Cheese every night. That was abouyt the extent of my Dad's culinary skills.

Even when she got better, I kept cooking. I love it, and this is a really great set-up for someone who likes to cook.
These are mostly hand-me-downs from Douglas and I to Taye. He gets most of his food from his job.

Well, he hasn't had my famous chicken diavolo, yet.
Mmm! Well, Taylor's a vegetarian, dear, but Douglas and I would love to taste it, I'm sure!

Is Douglas one of the other tenants?
Sort of, dear.
Douglas is my husband.

You didn't realize...?
I wasn't sure...

You first, dear.
Well...

I mean, I knew the ad was in Triangle Books, but I wasn't sure if that meant you were...
Well, I am. And so're the other tenants. I assume you are as well. Or else you just like hanging out in gay bookstores?

No, no. Heh. I'm gay. Taye too, hmm?
All of us. Doug and I on the top floor, Arthur in the basement.
Ken on the 2nd floor. It was his side door you paused at earlier.

The door on the left is the bathroom which you can check on your own, later.
The door on the right is the living room.
Shall we?

Taye used to live with his ex, Roger. They had a bit of a spat a few months ago. Roger stormed out, and Taye stayed.
He could afford to keep living on his own, but he wants to put some money aside, hence the ad.

This is the living room, obviously.
Nice.

Well, Arthur painted it. He's the downstairs tenant, and one of my oldest friends. He also refinished the basement and made a lovely studio down there.
This is really one of the nicest homes I've seen. It's almost like culture shock after living with my folks.

And here's the bedroom.

So...it's just the one bedroom?
Did we not say that in the ad?

Y'know, it probably did. But I never... y'know...stopped to think.
That you'd be sleeping in the same room as another gay man?
Right.

My dear Marty, it really is nothing to worry about. Taye is the very soul of propriety. He's a gentleman, and would never coerce you into anything untoward. And he's very pleasant company, besides.
Well, I mean, I'm sure he's nice.

Besides, in a college dorm, you never know what your roommates will be like. If they were homophobes, they'd be far worse to share with.
Oh, don't get me wrong. I really like the place, and the location. And the price is more than reasonable.
Heat, water, and friendly company are included as well.

Okay, I guess I'm officially interested. When would you be making a decision?
Well, so far, you're the only applicant...

Why don't we see if Arthur is home and introduce you to him? Based on some past experiences, I'd like to make sure that everyone is going to get along.
Drama, I don't need. I have plenty of my own.
Hehehe. Works for me.

Now, let's see if our "artist-in-residence" is currently in residence...

Arthur, dear, come up and meet the possible new tenant.
knock

Well, hey there. Arthur Korsky, professional basement lurker at your service.

Hi. I'm Marty Miller. Nice to meet you.

Arthur, is something...?
Oops! Tempus fugit! Excuse me one moment. Arthur, can you take young Marty here in hand?

Sure! C'mon, Marty. I'll give you the nickel tour.

Well, this is my lil corner of the house.
It isn't much to look at, but I like it this way. It's kind of my "Art Cave."

Wow, this is really good! Have you ever displayed your stuff, or sold your work?

Thanks. Glad you like it.
Nah, I'm not much for showing or selling my work. It's kinda personal. I sometimes give it to a friend, if someone sits for me.
You totally should! My Dad works at an art gallery. I bet I could help set up a show, if you wanted.
Maybe, if I get enough pieces together. Actually, though, I'd love it if you'd sit for me.

Me? Seriously? I didn't think I was art model material
Hey, if I only wanted to paint the body beautiful, I'd have Ken model all the time. I like lots of variation.
I also like more average models, with a little meat on the bones, as it were.

Well, I got that, I guess.
You and me both. Anyway, think about it. Might be fun.
Sure. Lemme think on it for a bit.

Yoo hoo! Am I missing all the fun?
I'm trying to lure young Martin here into an exciting life of non-mobility in the name of art.
Arthur wants me to model for him!

You should, dear. He's very good.
Well, when I have such good material...
Flatterer.

Oh? Did you ever sit for a painting, Paulie?

Many years ago, dear. When I was still young and hea...uh...handsome.

Is it still here somewhere?
It's upstairs, in our apartment.
Told you I gave some away.

Can I see it sometime?
Sometime, dear. Yes.

Before I forget, Paulie, I baked some bread for you.
Aha! I knew I smelled some down here. Lovely. I'll have some with a late lunch.

You'll stay for lunch, Marty?
Are you sure? I don't want to be a bother...
Don't be silly. I wouldn't have offered if you were a bother.
Then, sure! I'd love to.

Oh, it smells lovely.
I was going to bring it up, earlier, but I ran into Doug...

Is he still holding a grudge? I'll talk to him about it. Again.
Honestly. It isn't as if it were your fault.

HELLO? ANYONE HOME? I LOCKED MYSELF OUT OF MY APARTMENT!
ONE SEC, KEN! PAULIE AND I ARE BOTH DOWN HERE!
Whew! You're savin' my bacon, guys.
C'mon up and meet Ken.
Jeez, good thing you guys were home, Paulie. I can't believe I forgot my keys.

We all have our absent-minded days, dear.
By the by, this is Martin Miller, or just Marty. He might be our new tenant.

Hiya. Nice to meetcha. You'd be livin' with Taye, right?
So I hear.

He's a heckuva nice guy. Cute too. Dunno why he an' I never got together, y'know?
Uh, gee...I don't...hmmm.

You know perfectly well, Ken dear, that you two don't exactly see eye to eye on some key issues.
Monogamy, for instance?

Well, yeah, there is that. But, hey, I like t' play. Is that so bad? I'm careful. Where's the harm?

Maybe I'm not the best person to talk to about that.

Oh, Jeez...Paulie, I'm sorry. That was really bone-headed of me.

It's okay, Ken. Seems to be my day for it.
I'm really sorry, though. Didn't think before I said it.

It's okay, dear. Really. Tell you what. You can make it up by letting us detour through your apartment to get back upstairs.
Not a prob.

C'mon in, guys. It's a bit of a mess, but at least it's home.

No, it's really nice. I like your posters.
Thanks. I like to collect work by good photographers, when I can afford it.

Marty, dear, when you're ready, just come through the door in the kitchen. I'll be upstairs, fixing lunch.
'Kay, Paulie.
(You have *2* new messages.)

(Hi, Ken, it's Brian from the Gym. You gave me your number and said to call sometime.)
(So, if you wanna get together this weekend, give me a yell back. You've got my number. Would love to see you. Bye.)
BEEP

(Your message will be saved for...30 days. Next new message.)
Hey! You're in this book!
Was my first pro shoot. Great director. Very easy to work with.

(Ken, it's Alex. Look, I really think we need to talk. I know you said you didn't wanna see me no more, but didn't you think we had chemistry?)
Don't like it?

Just feel odd looking at naked pics of a guy I might be neighbors with.
I don't mind. Folks see 'em all the time.
(I know you have this whole love 'em an' leave 'em thing, but maybe we should explore more fully.)

Maybe another time?
Sure, and hey, I keep the inner door unlocked, if you ever wanna use my weights, or somethin'. Taye does, sometimes.
(Call me, okay? I really wanna...) *BEEP*

(Message deleted.)
Guess I could use some shaping up, huh?
Hey, some guys look good with a belly. But th' offer's on th' table.

Well, I might, at that.
Cool. Just, if th' door's locked, don't come a-knockin', y'know?
(End of messages.)
Visiting boyfriend?
Somethin' like that. Anyway, s'nice t' meetcha. Door's right through th' kitchen.
B

Hi. Oh, wow! You have the whole top floor, huh?
Yes, dear. Doug and I find it suits us perfectly. Now, do you like your toasted cheese sandwiches with or without tomato?

With, please.
A man after my own heart. And we have some lovely brownies...
BIOLOGY
T-Cells
Help for HIV
AIDS & YO
LIVING WITH

Paulie, can I ask you something?
Of course, dear. What is it?
Are you sick?
Oscar Wilde
IOLOGY
T-Cells
for HIV
AIDS & You
LIVING

Not exactly the best kept secret in the house, is it? Yes, dear. I'm HIV positive. Does that make you not want to rent? You can't catch it like a cold.
Oh, no! I love it here! I'm just sorry, is all.

Thank you, dear. I'm not wild about it myself, but I'm coping, as best I can.
I'm not meaning to pry. It's not like you look sick. You just have all these books.

And the stuff Ken and Arthur said. Does Arthur have it too?
No, dear! Why would you think that?

You said Doug blames Arthur for something...
Long story short, Arthur blames himself, because I caught it from a young man of his acquaintance.

Douglas holds him responsible, too, but in truth, it was my own fault. I got careless. I'm just sorry anyone I care about has to suffer, too.
Does Doug have it, too?
Not unless things have changed in the last month or so. He gets tested regularly.

So...do you two...do it?
Yes, dear. We don't do everything under the sun, but we still do a lot of things. We're just more careful than most people. *Much* more careful.
Do you know... how long?
Til the end of my lifetime. No more, no less.

That's a good way to think of it, I expect.
Keeps me going on the bad days.
RING, RING

Hello?
(Somebody's been sleeping in *my* bed.)

Hello, Taye, dear. Home from work?
(Yup. Is he still here?)

He is. Come up and join us for lunch? We're having grilled cheese and tomato sandwiches, with brownies for dessert.
(I'm on my way. I'll bring up this amazing pesto pasta salad we had at work today.)

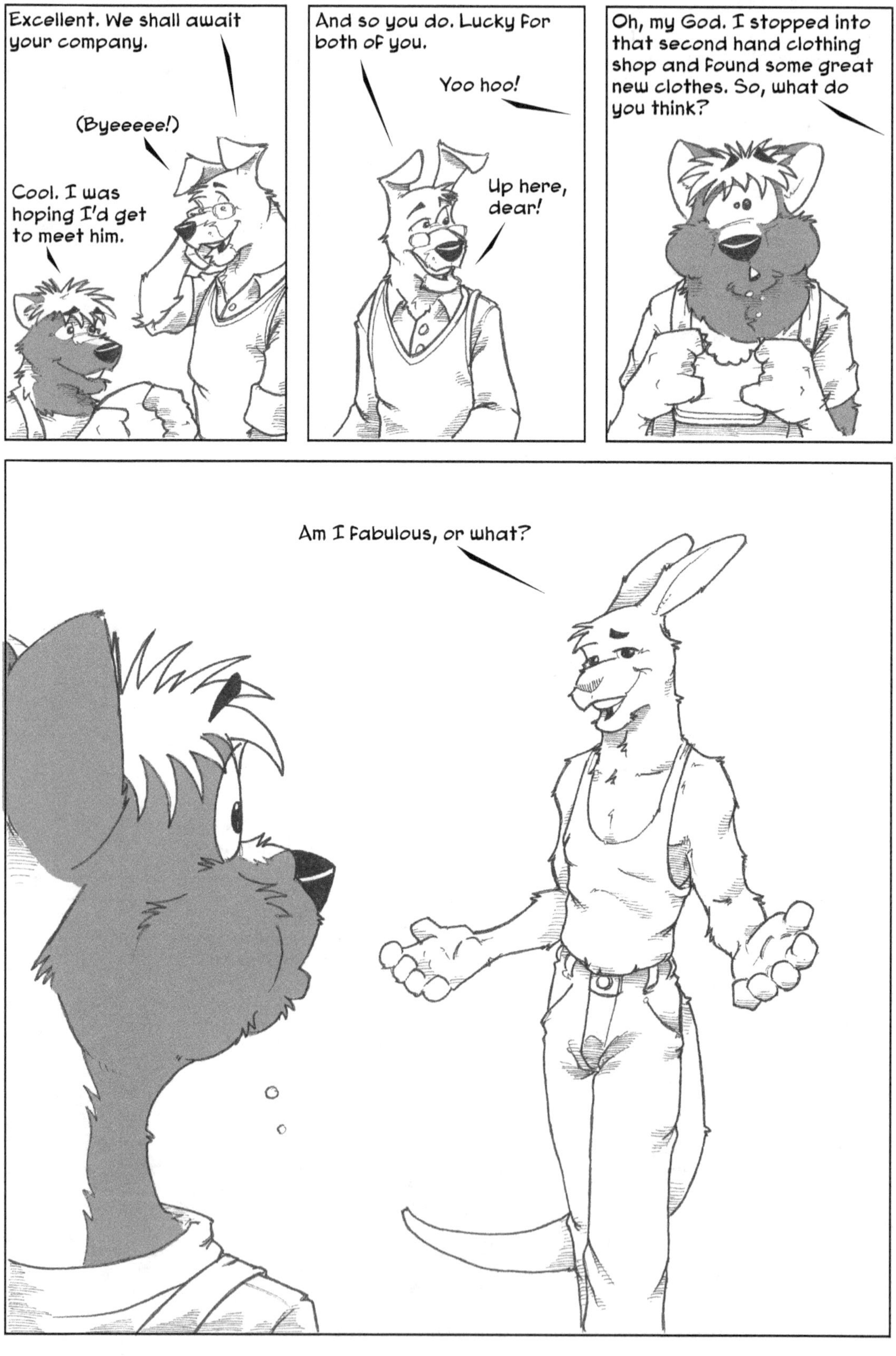

Am I fabulous, or what?

Quite a nice effect, dear. Don't you think so, Marty?

Swallow, dear. Breathe.

Wow! Those are amazing clothes! You sure know how to shop!

Oh, my! He's cute and complimentary! What a find! Where can I get one, Paulie?
If all goes well, quite possibly you'll find him in your bedroom.

Oo? Then we must make certain all goes well, n'est pas?
Wha?
That's French. It means 'is it not so?'

You speak French?
A touch. Mostly an inspired blend of French and English. Kind of like Pepe le Pew.

"Franglais."
Uhhhh...okay.

Try the pesto salad. It's yummy! Chef Louis makes just the best French dishes.
Pesto's Italian, dear.
Feh. That just means he's so brilliant, he cooks in different languages!

Of course. Pardon my interruption.
So, are you gonna take the apartment?
Well, I dunno yet. I really do like this place a lot...

Everyone here seems really nice, though I haven't met Douglas yet.
Oh, Douglas is a sweetie. I'm sure you'll get along with him.

But...well...the bedroom is a little small.
That bed is actually two beds stuck together. I can get used to sleeping in one again.
Well...

I'd still like you to meet Douglas first. He'll actually be here any time, now. But...well, if you're interested, Marty, I think I can safely say you'd fit right in with us. Now, if you two will excuse me a moment.
Of course. Thanks, Paulie.

So, Paulie says you went to B.U., too?
Guilty as charged. Graduated last year. Are you going there now? My condolences.

Last year? Well, maybe you knew my older brother, Alex? He graduated last year, too.
Well, I didn't meet too many folks outside the performing arts department to be honest.

Say, you're not nervous of me, are you?
Huh? N-nervous? Me? That's silly.

W-well...hmmm...maybe a little.

Thought so. Look, Marty...I think you're really cute, and I know I come on kind of strong, but I'm not gonna jump your bones while you're asleep.
I didn't think that.
Sure you did. And believe me, it's tempting. You're a sexy guy.

Aw, you're teasing me. But that's okay.
No, I'm not. Honestly. I think you're seriously cute.

Really?
Cross my heart.

Omigod! You're blushing! That's so cute! I can't believe it! I didn't think anyone blushed any more.
Well, you're not helping matters any.

Look, not every gay guy thinks Ken is the definition of hot. Don't sell yourself short. You're a really cute guy.
No one ever said I was cute before.

Oh? You're not gonna tell me you're a virgin or something?
Well...no. Not exactly.

Whoops! I'm not stirring up a hornet's nest?
No. I just haven't done too much, and the guy I was with was kind of a jerk. There's a lot of stuff I haven't tried yet, and...this is really personal. Why am I telling you all this? I just met you.

It's a gift I have. People open up to me. But, hey, let's leave it there. If you move in, you can tell me when you're comfortable. If you don't move in, you won't have told embarrassing secrets to a stranger.
I think I'd like to move in, actually. The place is great. You guys are nice. So why not? Assuming Paulie's cool with it.

As long as Doug is cool, Paulie'll be cool, I think. And I can't imagine why Doug wouldn't be cool.
Okay, I'm back. You have to stop talking about me behind my back, now.
We'll have to start talking about you in front of your back.

We're not even talking about you, you egotistical old queen. We're talking about Marty and whether he's going to move in.
Well, I assume Doug will be okay with it.
I'm assuming it's okay with you, Taylor, dear?

Perfectly okay with me! What do you say?
Well, I'd like to talk to my folks, but...aw, what the heck. If Douglas says he's cool, then I'd love to live here.
Then we're just waiting on Doug.

Waiting for me on what? Something good, I hope?
Oh, you're home!

Mmmmm...

Hi, you must be Martin Miller. Douglas Pope. Call me Douglas or Doug. Whichever is fine.
Marty, please, Doug.

So, did your feeling turn out correct?
Well, Arthur and Ken both seem okay with him. And Taye's practically molesting the poor thing...
Not that he seems to mind.

So it's mostly your input we need.
I trust everyone's judgement, of course... but does he like my brownies?
Try one.

Whoa! These're awesome.
He's in.
Yes!

Dear Douglas,

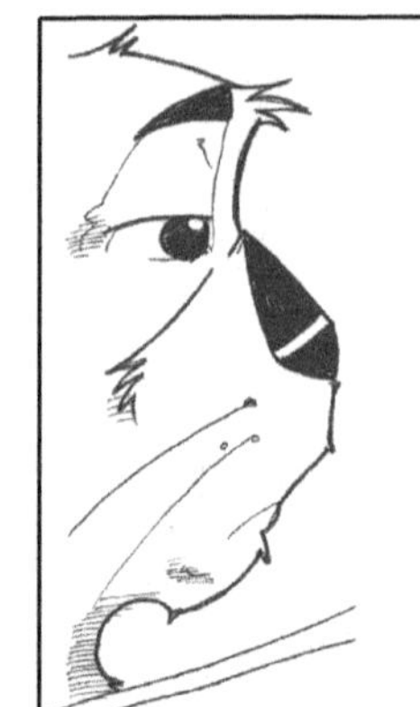

Well, it has been quite a day. I'm sure that Marty will work out fine as a tenant, and I think Taye is already sweet on him.

I wonder...how will that come out?

Only time will tell, I suppose.

There's something about new love... especially young love...that makes me feel young again.

But then, there's something about loving you that makes me feel the same. How does the song go?

"Something about sharing;
Something about always."

I'm worried about your feelings for Arthur. He's a good man, Douglas, and I really wish you could see that what happened wasn't his fault at all. I made a bad decision, and I have to live with the consequences of that.

Ken worries me, too. He just doesn't take AIDS seriously enough. It's as if he's convinced he'll be fine no matter what, and I'm scared he'll make his own foolish decision someday. I hope I can convince him before it's too late.

I know my being sick hurts you, but it isn't right to punish Arthur for it. I just wish he'd stop acting so damned guilty about it. It's hard to convince you he's innocent when he doesn't truly believe it himself.

Everyone is so happy tonight. We're celebrating a new beginning. Everyone seems happy to set aside the cares of everyday life to celebrate the start of something new. I wonder where this fresh start will take us. I womder if I'll be here to see the ending.

But that's just foolishness, isn't it?

There are no beginnings or endings. This is just another point along the circle my life has always been. There are always new people that enter your life, for good or for ill, and then leave again, at some later, undetermined point. Some of them are just short spins along the circle's arc, while others go round and round with you as the years fly past.

On the other hand, perhaps I'm just a pretentious old queen who's been listening to too much Harry Chapin of late.

In any case, it's late, and I want to curl up in bed with you. I love you, very, very much. I don't know why you stay...why you put up with me when you could have any healthy man in the world...
But I'm glad you stay.

I really don't know what I would do without you. Sometimes the only way I can get to sleep at night is knowing you'll be there in the morning.

I hope you stay with me for always.

However long that is.

I will always love you.

Love, Paulie

circles

Circles Issue 2

Introduction by Andrew French

Issue 2 is set in early summer to late summer of 2001. The title, of course, is from the Beatles' song "Do You Want to Know a Secret," which is, in turn, based on the song "I'm Wishing" from Disney's Snow White. No joke!

This issue didn't need much editing. But we had to change Paulie's journal font to bring it in line with the rest of the series. I guess we had to play around to find fonts we liked. The font we used looked more like actual handwriting, but it was hard to read.

The Urban Peasant was a wacked-out cooking show that was on our local cable channel when I was writing it. And yes, he did make garbage pail stew, in an actual garbage can, and it did involve apricots.

I loved Mrs. Nussbaum from the moment I started writing her, and her quirky way of speaking is a lot of fun to work on when she appears in the book, as is her semi-acerbic yet loving relationship with Doug. We also mention Carter Allen in this issue, who won't show up until Issue 3. To my embarrassment, I realized later that Carter Allen is the name of a D.J. on a local classic rock station. Mr. Allen, if you ever read this, sorry 'bout that!

The whole "It's peach, dear," gag is from The Desert Peach, by Donna Barr. It's my nod to a wonderful book, and you may notice some slight resemblances between Paulie and Pfirsch if you know both books.

Paulie's coming out story is a true story from our friend Dan Markey. It made us all laugh, and we begged him to let us include it in the book. He graciously consented, and you'll see Scott's drawing of his character in the night club scene in Issue 2.

Marty's grandmother is based on my father's mother (although my family isn't Jewish), and some of her quotes (including her last line) are based on stuff my Grammy has actually said to and about me. Fun woman that... not!

Since Circles is based in part on real life, Marty's coming out is sort of a hyper-exaggerated version of my own coming out. In reality, I told my Mom I was bi at first, and she replied, "Really? I thought you were gay." Moms know, I think. At least mine did. And she loves the comic. Hi, Mom!

Dear Douglas
Dear

How're you? I hope that, wherever and whenever you read this, you are well.
It's a gorgeous summer day; beach weather, as it were. The kind of day that makes you think of the ocean, picnics, and play.

Marty is moving in, today, and we're meeting his family for the first time. I'd better go greet them before taye scares them half to death. I gather Marty's parents are rather comservative. Bye for now.
CRASH

Hello, Marty! So good to see you back!
Hiya, Paulie. Good to see you, too. This is exciting!

And you must be Mr. Miller. Welcome!
Thank you, Mr. Mayhew. Marty's had a lot to say about you and this house. You must've made quite an impression on him.

Dad...
Please call me Paulie, Mr. Miller. No one calls me anything else, really... and the good first impressions were mutual in Marty's case. He's a charming boy.

Wait! Must catch the moment on film. Everyone say cheese!

Circles

Listen. Do You Want to Know a Secret?

Hiya. Mind if I join you?
Not at all.
Thanks. I could use a break from polite company.

Gee, thanks so much.
Oops! *giggle* I didn't mean it like that. Sorry.

Forget about it. What's going on anyways?
Marty's folks are dropping him and his stuff off today.
Right. It's the big day. Sorry to be losing your private apartment?

Oh, a little, I suppose. But it'll be worth it, with the money I'll be able to put away.
Yeah, I guess. But you still have to live with Marty.
I like Marty. He's sweet, thoughtful...

Oh, yeah. Hes a nice enough guy, but you couldve gotten a nicer-looking guy.
Hey! Mr. Superficial! I happen to think that Martys a pretty cute guy.
For a chubby guy, you mean?
No, in general. I think chubby guys are sexy. There's more of them to hug!

Ohhhh. Now I get it.
Get what?
I could never figure out why we never got together. You're a chubby chaser.

So, Ken, who're you going out with these days? That Cliff guy? Or is it Barrett?
Norris, actually. Why?

Who's Norris?
He's new. You haven't met him.

When did you break up with Barrett?
Which one was Barrett?
The guy from your gym. About a week ago?

I thought that was Cliff?

That's why we never got together.

Oh yeah! Cliff was the hottie with the red sportscar, right?

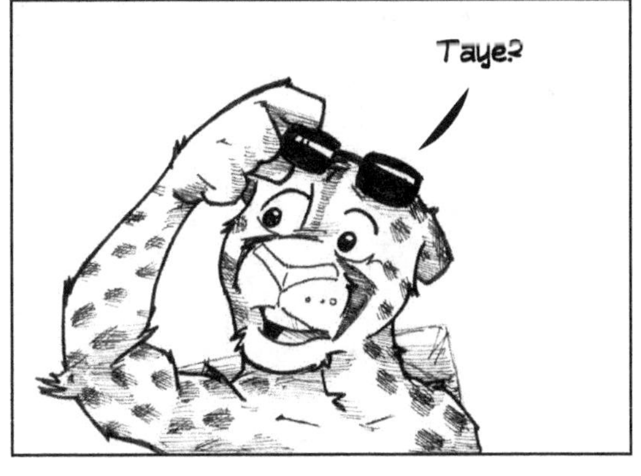
Taye?

Your parents seem like a charming couple, Marty. I hope they're adjusting to the idea of you moving out?
Me too. Dad looked kind of freaked when he saw the one bed, but I told him we'd be pulling them apart today.

I wonder if he figured out that you and Taye are gay.
Well, if he didn't, then he's in denial. Taye and I aren't exactly subtle.

I wonder if he's thinking I am, then.
You haven't told them?

There just never seemed a good time to do it. My folks're pretty right wing about a lot of stuff. I don't know if I'll ever tell them.

Marty, your parents love you. I could see that right off. No matter what, they're going to love you, whether you're gay, straight, bi, or whatever.

But what if Dad freaks out? Tells me I'm not his son any more? Or my Mom has a crying jag, or something? I dunno if I could handle that.
That's a bit extreme, no? Besides if your parents are at all observant, they may already suspect, or know. You don't particularly come across as gay, but parents... well.. sometimes parents just know.

Think that's why my Mom gave me this pink shirt last Hannukah?
That's not pink, dear. It's peach. Pink is tacky.

Need any help in here, or can I shirk a bit longer?
You can take over for an old man. I need to pay some bills. And Marty? Why don't we invite your parents over to dinner next weekend? Taye can bring home some nice things from La Maison, you could make something good, and Douglas and I could make some dessert.

Thanks, Paulie. That'd be cool. At least my Mom would be able to see that I was eating okay.
Oh, she needn't fear, I think.
Be good, boys.

So what were you and the esteemed Mr. Mayhew talking about, hmmm?
Oh... my folks, mostly. I haven't come out to them, and I'm a little worried about what they're thinking about me moving in here with you.

Yeah, I thought your Dad looked kind of... uncomfortable when he saw just the one bed. But we'll get Arthur up here to help us pull em apart.
You think he suspects you now?

I don't know. I don't even know if I care. I mean, I'd like my family to really know who I am, but, if they don't, is that really going to matter to anyone?
Well turn that around. What if you meet someone that you fall so much in love with that you want to spend the rest of your life with them? Be a shame if your parents never knew you were married, so to speak.

Well, I just don't know. I don't want to cause friction. What if one of them freaks out, and the other doesn't?
Then one of your parents has a problem. Who do you think would freak? Your Dad?

Yeah, I love him, but he can get very uptight about some stuff, and I worry this'll... I dunno... really be bad for him.
Send him over the edge into a nervous breakdown or a heart attack or something?

No, no. I... oh, I don't know. Let's not worry about it. I'm gonna get my computer set up.
Scool. I gotta split for work anyhow. If you get a chance, you can ask Arthur to come up and help you with the beds. He helped me fix them together in the first place.

Okay, Taye. Thanks for your help.

Explain to me again what he's making?
Garbage Pail Stew.
"Now this is going to make it really lovely..."

But he just added Apricots!?
You question the Urban Peasant?

None of us would dare, dear. Just please don't cook whatever it is he's making.
Hey! I just watch him to get a feel of what can be done.

As long as it remains hypothetical.
Philistine.

So we're set for Saturday?
Yes, dear. Taye assures me there is an exquisite beef and noodle dish being prepared at La Maison, and he's promised enough for ten. What are you making, dear?

A sour cream and potato dish. Veggies for Taye.
Not exactly kosher, but my family plays it loose.
As long as you're sure, dear.

And what are we making, Douglas?
We? Aren't you afraid I'll slip some apricots in?

Don't be silly. You could cook rings around the Urban Peasant any day.
Well... That's true. Honesty must be rewarded. How about some kind of chocolate pudding cake?

YOO HOO!
ANYONE HOME?
Mrs. Nussbaum!

Mrs. Nussbaum?
We're up here, Mrs. Nussbaum! Won't you come up and join us?

Oh, boys. Something smells sooo good!
It's the clam sauce for the linguine.
Ach. Good-smelling, then, but it can stay with the smelling. Ah, Paulie, dear, How're you?

In the pink, Mrs. N. Allow me to introduce Marty Miller.
Marty, this is Mrs. Nussbaum who lives just down the street.

Ah, Marty Miller. A pleasure to finally meet you. Paulie's told me all about you.
Very nice to meet you, Mrs. Nussbaum.

Ach, such nice manners. Finally a bit of class in the house.
Lovely to see you, too, Mrs. N.

Don't go putting words in my mouth. Sometimes the boys youve had here, they were not quite so nice looking as Mr. Marty Miller here.
Too true, Mrs. N. Too true.

So youre gay of course, Marty? I know the boys who come to live here, theyre gay. And thats fine.
Thats us, Mrs. N.

When Paulie first moved in, thirty years ago, my Herman, rest his soul swore hed never live on the same street as fagelehs.
But were such happy fagelehs, Mrs. N.

When you call yourself gay, what else should you be?
Too true, Mrs. N. Too true.

Most of us know, of course, that youre just people. And some of you nice people who have lots to share.
Baking recipes.

Teasing, always. But still good friends.

As you have always been to us. And this is one of your famous welcomes?
Just a little something. A sponge cake.

For me? Aw, thanks, Mrs. Nussbaum.
Just a little welcome gift.
Which is big enough to feed Africa...

Ach. Someone isn't tending to his clams and sauce.
Nyah!

Well, boys I can't stay. I have to pick my grandson, Joshua, up from band practice. Such a very great pleasure, Marty Miller.
Be good, Paulie. Take care of yourself.
Always, Mrs. N.

And Paulie? Make sure Douglas takes care of his clams and sauce.
Yes, Mrs. N. Will do.

Such a remarkable woman. If I were straight...
She's the best. Wish more folks in the neighborhood were like her...
Carter Allen for one...

She seems really nice, and really accepting. Speaking of which, you know I'm thinking more and more about coming out to my folks.

I think that´s the best idea, Marty. My mother died when I was a teenager, and I always regretted never getting a chance to tell her. So, just before I left for America, I told my Dad. I wanted him to realize that I love him, and for him to know who I was.
Did that go well?

It went well enough. But you have to imagine this tall hulk of a man weeping because his own bonny boy is going away to America...to be a homosexual, no less.

Jeez.

Well, Arthur says he doesn't have the right tool to pull the beds apart. So I guess we have to sleep with the beds together...at least for tonight.
That's okay. I don't mind the closeness...

Unless it bothers you?
Not really, I guess. Arthur says he can fix it this weekend.

No problem, then.
Okay. Gonna brush my teeth.
I'll alert the media.
Huh? Oh...heh. Yeah.

Did you used to wear that sweatshirt to bed at home?
Huh?

Was that what you wore for p.j.s back home?
Well...no. I didn't really used to wear anything.

Well, we're roomies, Marty. Whether our beds are together, or not, there's nothing wrong with sleeping naked in the same room, right?
Um...no...not really. But since the beds are together...I thought you'd prefer...?
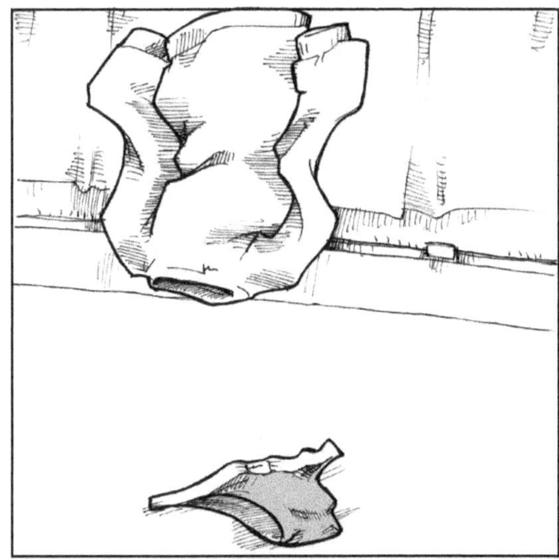

All set with the lights?
Sure.

Well...good night.
Night.
"CLICK"

Marty...
I'm sorry! I can't help it! I'm not used to sleeping in bed with someone! Especially naked!
I can't help fidgeting! I think I snore, too! You must hate me!

Whoa! Relax, Marty!

Actually, I was gonna ask if you minded if I put my arm around and snuggled up.
Um...no?

Mmmmm...You're comfy. All warm and snuggly. Like a teddy bear...
And so cute...

I'm cute?
Very cute. Night, Marty.
Night, Taye.

(I'm cute!)

DING-DONG

They're heeeeeere.
Oh, God!

It'll be fine, dear.
Want me to get it?
Don't be silly, Taye. Marty wants to answer the door as Master of his own home. Don't you, Marty?

Uh-oh. Meltdown.
Oh, God.
Uh...maybe you should get it, Taye.

N-no...
I'll get it.

Poor Marty. He seems so flustered.
Yeah, I mean, what could go wrong? It's just dinner with his folks.

Oh, God!

Hi, Mom. Hi, Dad. Hi...

G-grandma?!

Hello, Martin, dear.
You look...well.

It's a...nice surprise
to see you, Grandma.
Won't you all
come in?

Thank you, Marty.
Nice shirt,
son. Pink
suits you.

It's not pink.
It's peach.

Well, um...Mom, Dad, you already met Paulie and Taye. And...that's Douglas, who's helping me cook.
And...um...everyone, some of you met my Mom and Dad. And this...this is my Grandma.

Well, hello! We weren't expecting you, but you're most certainly welcome.
Oh, why thank you, young man.

Please, call me Paulie. Everyone does.
And you must call me Francine.

Pleasure to see you again, Mr. Miller.
Likewise, Taye.
Just gonna check on dinner...

Oh my God! What are we gonna do?
What? What's wrong?

My Grandmother is a lot stricter than the rest of us. She eats kosher! She's just this side of demanding two sets of dishes!
Erk!

That means the beef is out...because the sauce has sour cream in it.
So do the potatoes. And the pudding cake has milk...

Well, that's okay, because it's a seperate course. But the rest...oh, God! Why did they they have to bring Grandma?
Don't panic. I've got plenty of food upstairs. You entertain them while I run up and figure out what we're having.

Right. Thanks, Douglas.
No problem. And don't worry. I saw this once on "The Urban Peasant".

WHAT?!
Joke, Marty.

If I survive this, remind me to hate you.
Will do!

Dinner will be served in just a teensy bit.

There's my favorite grandson.
Hi, Grandma.

Take my seat, Marty.
I'll just pop in to keep Douglas company.
When do I get my kiss? I didn't get my kiss.

I hope you don't mind me inviting myself along at the last minute.
Course I don't. How've you been, Grandma?

Good, good. Well, not so well, you know, but okay. Wondering when I'll have great grandkids.
Uh...

Speaking of which, when are you going to find someone and settle down, Marty?
I dunno, Grandma. When I meet the right person, I guess.

Well, until you lose some weight, who knows when that'll happen.
Grandma...

Marty, you could be the handsomest boy in the family. You could have your pick of any girl. But you've got to lose some weight first. You will never get a pretty girl until you lose some weight. This is not good!

but...I'm cute...

Yo, folks.
Howdy, Marty.
Oh, hi guys! Everyone, this is Ken and Arthur.

How's it hangin', Mr. Miller?
Excuse me?
Sorry we're late. We were picking up wine, and I'm pretty picky, especially with reds.

Arthur, could you coordinate the wine with Paulie and Douglas...in the kitchen?
But, Marty, this is one of the best reds on the market...
We might not need red...
Huh?
Douglas can explain.

So what do you do for work, Mr. Miller?
Well, I do some work with art galleries...
Oh yeah? Any photo exhibitions? I ve been in a few photo shoots for artists...

Really? Anything I might've seen?
Oh, I kinda doubt it...
Why is this happening to me?

Everything okay out here?
Not really! What are we gonna...?

Tonight's menu consists of an exquisite ginger-chicken stir-fry, served over a bed of noodles. Dessert is a chocolate pudding cake, which, even now, is bubbling in the oven.
Arthur's on his way to buy some white wine, and he promised to run all the way.

So, go spend quality time with your family and leave the rest to your fairy godfathers.
But...
But what?

Nothing. Thank you all. You guys are the best.
No problem, dear. Try to relax, okay?
I'll try.

Everything going okay? I hope I haven't caused any fuss. I could help out, if they need me.
No, Grandma. They're all set. They don't need any help.

Just think, Marty. Someday it'll be you and your wife scurrying around, getting things ready.
Jeez, Grandma! I dont even have a girlfriend! Maybe I dont want to get married?

What? Why ever not?
Well, maybe I'm... maybe I just... dont want to.

You're just young, dear. Someday, you'll find the right girl, and you'll want to settle down.
No, Grandma...I don't think so.
Oh! Don't be so silly, Marty. Of course you will!

I'm not being silly, I'm just...oh, never mind.
Of course you're being silly, Marty. Who wouldn't want to get married?

What's all the fuss over here?
Oh, Marty's just being silly.
I'm not being silly! I just don't want to get married!

You don't want to get married? Why not?
Oh, Ralph. Marty's still so young.
Mom, please. I'm not that young. I just dont want to marry anyone.
See? Isnt that silly?

Uh-oh. I think Marty's feeling ganged-up on...
Maybe we should rescue him?

Well, my neighbor, Mrs. Eckhardt? She has a lovely grand-daughter, just about your age. I have her number here, someplace...
Grandma, I'm not interested!

We'd better intervene. Marty looks like he's about to blow.
Mmm...

But you don t even know her, yet. How could you know whether or not you d be interested in her?
Because...because I'm gay, Grandma.
What? What? Did you say you're a goy?

I said I'm gay, Grandma! Okay? I'm gay! I'm not interested in girls! At all! I like guys! And only guys!
I'm a lot more interested in Taye than I am in Mrs. Eckhardt's grand-daughter.
Okay? Okay? Are you happy?
No need to shout, dear.

Oh, dear.

You're...gay?

Mom, Dad...yes. I'm sorry. This isn't how I wanted to tell you. But everything went wrong tonight, and...it all just kind of got away from me.
But, yes. What I said is true. I'm gay.

You're sure? No interest in girls at all?
I'm sure. I have no real interest in girls.

Pay up, Ralph.
What?!
Damn.

I don't understand. You...you had a bet? On whether or not I was gay?

Something like that. Your Dad just refused to believe me, but I knew you were gay.
You...you did?
Marty, honey, I'm your mother. Of course I knew.

But...Dad? You didn't?
I think I just didn't want you to be. I thought maybe you were bi, but I guess that was wishful thinking.
Huh?
Well...if you were bi, I could at least hope for grandkids.

I'm going to lie down and go insane, now, if no one minds.
Honey, we're your parents. We've known you all your life. It was kind of obvious...
That I was gay?

That you weren't interested in girls. Remember Sarah? You took her to the prom, and then ducked her calls for days afterwards. That started me thinking...
Guess that makes sense.

So, after seeing that kind of thing for a few years, we got to know there was something special about you. If this is who you are, then this is who you are. But remember, honey, we love you, and we just want you to be happy.

That's right, Marty.

Thank God that's over.
Definitely one of the more memorable dinner parties I've ever been to.
I'm not likely to forget it, any time soon.

But how do you feel?
I feel good. I'm glad I told them. Just wish it coulda gone a bit more smoothly.

But...?
Weight of the world off my shoulders.

So...did you mean it?
Mean what?
You said you were interested in me.

More than in Mrs. Eckhardt's daughter, sure.
Tease.

Yes, I'm interested in you.
Well, I'm interested in you, too.

Yeah?
Well, sure. I think you re the nicest guy Ive met in a long time...
and I really do think you re cute.

No one ever called me cute before.
No one?

Well, the only guy I've been with before was this guy called Larry. My friend Ed set me up with him, mostly to get Larry off his own back. So Larry was trying to get closer to my friend by getting closer to me.
Once he succeeded in getting my friend into bed, I was pretty much dumped by the curb.
I didn't think Larry loved me, but I thought he at least liked me.

Marty...I'm so sorry. That's horrible I would never do that to anyone. Especially not you!
I know you wouldn't, Taye. You're a really nice guy, too.

Well, I'm not 100% nice...
No? What have you done that was bad?

Well...I bribed Arthur to pretend he couldn't pull the beds apart...
Really? You bad boy!

Sure am.
Wanna
spank me?

Heh...no, that's okay.
I forgive you.

Would you like to go out with me sometime, Marty?
Like...on a date?
Yes. On a date.

Yeah. I'd like that a lot. But, can we go slow?
Of course we can.

It may sound old-fashioned, but I'm looking for...well...the right guy.
I'd like that, too. And I hope he's as cute and as nice and as sexy as you.

You know...I've only known you a short time, but I think you may be the best friend I ever had.
Well...that's a good place to start.

Well Douglas, all things considered, Marty's dinner party didn"t go to badly.

For better or for worse, he's out to his family, now, and they seemed to take it very well. And if their reaction wasn't exactly what he expected, well...
At least they didn't throw him out, or disown him or any other nonsense.
Grandma seemed a trifle upset. Oh well.
She has three other grandkids to badger.

At least everyone enjoyed the cocolate pudding cake.

Hi there, handsome.
Hi, yourself.

Writing in your journal?
Well, I was...

So, when do I get to read it?
Later.

But... what if I don't want to wait til later?
Well, you're going to have to

You're here in bed with me now, and being a goober as usual...
Wanna play?

Ah...apparently, you're frisky, so I'm going to sign off.
I would love to, as long as we're careful. Do we have supplies?

We have plenty of condoms...and plenty of lube.
Sounds like a good start.

Take care of yourself, my love.

Love Paulie

6 Kinsey Circle

With the Moon Keeping Watch Over Me

Introduction by Andrew French

I was asked to write a piece for the conbook for Feral, an extremely enjoyable summer-camp style convention that Steve and I were the guests of honor at. I was originally going to set it between issues 6 and 7, but then I realized that I would have to drop some BROAD hints in about future plot to do so, so I decided to set it between 2 and 3. It's just a little character piece.

With the Moon Keeping Watch Over Me

By Andrew French

Dear Douglas,

I honestly can't tell you the last time I went camping, but I think it may have been with my father on one of those rare occasions when he wanted to act the way he felt a "proper family" should. My memories are not completely unpleasant, but they certainly don't compare with the wonderful time I've had on this trip. What a very enjoyable weekend! I'm not certain what time it is, but I believe it's extremely early. I woke up with a bit of a cramp, so I've just nipped out here to the picnic table to do a little bit of writing by the light of the Coleman lantern. Beastly things, these cramps. I'm glad the doctor isn't concerned by them, but they're a bloody nuisance, I don't mind saying.

As I write this, I can hear Arthur snoring softly; I can't believe John is able to sleep through that racket. Marty and Taye's tent is quiet, though they were giggling softly not all that long ago. Ken doesn't seem to be in his tent, so I think he may be down in the boathouse by the lake with that fellow from two campsites down… again. Randy lads. I'm stunned by how long Ken's been with Michael now, but I'm afraid to bring it up for fear of ruining things, somehow. You were sleeping peacefully when I slipped out to the loo, and you still seem to be, which I'm thankful for. I just don't want you to wake up and start worrying.

I think I may take a bit of a walk myself, see if I can stretch out the cramps. I'll leave you a note so you won't "wig out" when you wake up. I'm looking forward to one more canoe ride tomorrow… well, later today I should say… before we have to drive back.

Thank you, my love. Thank you for everything.

Love, Paulie

* * *

Paulie sighed and cracked his back. It's bad enough being ill, he thought to himself. It's a damned nuisance to have to get old as well. The doctor had told him that the cramping in his gut was little more than a bit of gastroenteritis, and there was no need to call off the camping trip for it, as long as he didn't mind frequent trips to the W.C. He had no intention of calling off the trip, since it had been his idea in the first place. And he was able to blame the frequent rest-stops on a bit of fussy stomach, so Douglas wasn't worrying too badly.

He made his way down to the shoreline and admired the stillness of the lake. It was stirred only by a light breeze, and he could see the full moon reflected in it brightly. Across the lake, at another campsite, someone had a bonfire going, and he could make out a few forms around it. The occasional laugh and squeal told him it was a family, up late, probably having as much fun as his family had been having a few hours before. He smiled, softly, and walked along, humming to himself. Ecstatic sounds from the boathouse told him that it was indeed occupied by his housemate and some young man, and he idly wondered if it was, indeed, the wiry fellow from two campsites down, or some new fling. He caught himself smiling, just a touch envious of Ken's ability to play without fear. He just hoped his friend would sober up a bit before anyone got seriously hurt, physically, emotionally, or otherwise.

He found his steps taking him up the forested hill, towards the watch tower that offered such lovely views of the nearby White Mountains during the day. He hadn't really felt like climbing it with the others, earlier, but now he really wished to. He paused at the base of it, surprised to find the gate open. He looked up. According to the placard he'd read earlier, the open-topped tower had been built by the Park Services commission as a look-out point for forest fires prior to more sophisticated tracking and reporting systems. The full moon enticed him upwards, and he found himself slowly ambling up the uneven stone steps to the top. It's a wonder they don't lock it at night, he thought, idly. Someone could fall and injure themselves in the dark.

At the top, he collapsed onto one of the provided benches. Although the night was cool, he felt hot and winded, and he grumbled at himself for making the ridiculous excursion. What if you fell, you old fool? That'd be a fine thing. Oh, no, Doug, my T-Cells are surprisingly good today, but, oh dear, I've broken my leg. Give us a hand to the car? He shook his head… then looked up to the moon. It seemed bigger here, and he felt more naked under it, for all that he was fully dressed. He shivered, slightly, but not because it was cold.

"Quite a sight, isn't it?" said a voice, and he jumped. He saw Taye's smiling face from the area of the stairs. "Sorry, Paulie. I saw your note when I got up to hit the toilet, and I thought you wouldn't mind some company. I didn't mean to scare you."

"Oh, Taye dear… you just startled me is all." He patted the bench. "Please, join me."

Taye sat down next to the older man and patted his knee, fondly.

"You okay, Paulie? Bad dream? Or just can't sleep?"

Paulie smiled, wryly. "No bad dreams… haven't quite made it to sleep yet. Stomach's been giving me some troubles. Nothing serious, but not exactly conducive to a good night's rest, even when cradled on a comfy air mattress."

"Yeah, those mattresses John brought are great! I was a little worried about getting a root in the back, but we're both sleeping pretty comfortably." Taye flicked a pebble off the bench. "Hey, Paulie… can I ask you something?"

Paulie perked. "Hm? Oh, of course, dear. What is it?"

Taye looked down at his feet. "Well… what do you think of Marty?"

Paulie chuckled. "I think he's a lovely boy, dear. And I'm very pleased that you two are getting on so well. Why? Is there a problem? I thought you two were… well… becoming something of an item."

Taye blushed a little and nodded. He ran a finger over the bench's rough wood. "I think we are, too. But I'm a little nervous of it. I mean, he's never been in a real serious relationship before, from what he's told me. He's still very young… what if he finds someone else?"

Paulie pondered Taye's face. There was something on it he'd never seen before; he looked afraid. "Taylor Dooley," Paulie said, with a chuckle, "you surprise me. You've never struck me as someone to doubt what his heart is telling him. What is it telling you about Marty?"

Taye blushed even deeper, but the troubled look remained. "I think Marty's adorable, and he's certainly as sweet and thoughtful as I could ever hope for. But he's shy, too, and nervous about sex. I promised him we'd take it very slow, and you know I don't mind waiting… but…."

Paulie smiled and patted Taye's hand, gently. "But you're a horny fellow who knows what he wants, and who won't mind waiting for it… but wishes he knew what the final outcome would be?"

Taye sighed. "It's that obvious, huh? I mean, what if Marty ultimately decides I'm not the guy for him? I know Arthur and John are both pretty taken with him, too, and he's admitted he finds them both attractive. What if he decides to be with one of them, instead of me? Or someone he hasn't even met yet?"

"Well," Paulie said, after they were both quiet a moment. "You have a couple of points in your favor. Firstly, at least he knows he's gay, and his family is supporting him in it. Doug and I didn't have things quite that easy, but it was a slightly different time."

Taye frowned. "I can't imagine going through that. If Marty's family had reacted like Doug's did, it would've crushed him. And I know he keeps ties with Linda, but that must have all been horribly awkward."

Paulie chucked, softly, nodding. "Yes, I doubt I'll ever exactly be on Linda's Christmas Card list. I think she still thinks I stole him away. And, given the circumstances, I can't blame her for not being particularly thrilled with either of us."

"You said there was more than one point in my favor?"

"Well, I've seen the way Marty looks at you, when you aren't looking at him," Paulie said, with a wink. "Trust me, he doesn't look at either John or Arthur that way." Paulie put an arm around Taye's shoulders. "You bring something out in Marty that I don't think even he realized was there. You make him brave and funny and sexy and smart. I doubt anyone's ever made him feel like that, and it's not a feeling he's likely to give up for a physical infatuation."

Taye nodded, thinking for a few moments. "When did you know that Doug was… y'know… 'The One.'"

Paulie thought about that. "Well… I definitely knew when we kissed for the first time. There was no question at all."

Taye laughed. "Just like the song, huh? It's in his kiss?"

Paulie snickered. "Shoop, shoop."

Taye giggled softly, leaning into the older man's side. Then he sighed. "We haven't kissed, yet…." He grinned. "We do sleep naked together, though. That's a good thing, right?"

Paulie chuckled in surprise. "Do you? Oh my. But no improprieties, I trust?"

Taye smiled. "I'm being good, honestly. I just want him to feel good about his body, so I coaxed him into it. I think he's so sexy; I just wish he could see it."

"He will. Just be patient with him. I sincerely believe he'll reward your patience and effort."

Taye kissed Paulie's cheek. "Thanks, Paulie… thank God you're here. I couldn't go to my Dad for advice on these things."

Paulie grinned. "Glad to fill in, as it were. How are your folks, by the way?"

Taye shrugged. "The same. They're still being nice and distant and polite. They keep saying my being gay doesn't concern them, but I think they're just as happy I live as far away as I do. They don't want to know anything about Marty, or my day-to-day life, or who I'm living with, or anything. Their loss, as far as I'm concerned. Marty's parents couldn't be nicer; I've had dinner with them a few times, now."

Paulie patted Taye's shoulder. "Well, that's good, at least, dear."

Taye yawned. "Well, thanks for talking, Paulie. I do feel a bit better. How about you?"

Paulie felt his stomach. "I think my cramps have called a truce for now." He smiled, softly. "Helping other people always makes me forget my own troubles, anyway. I'm going to stay up a little longer."

Taye smiled as he stood up. "Well, don't stay up too late. Remember, Doug and I are gonna show off all our boy scout cooking techniques tomorrow."

Paulie chuckled. "Scrambled eggs cooked in a paper bag. The mind boggles and the stomach heaves."

Taye giggled. "Don't worry… I brought some extra peanut butter and jelly, just in case."

"Well, there's your boy scout training," Paulie chuckled. "Be prepared."

Taye flashed Paulie the traditional Scout three-fingered salute and giggled, then headed down the stairs. Paulie remained there, gazing out over the water, admiring the way the full moon shone down, painting everything in pale, washed-out colors. He saw Taye emerge from the tower's base and walk back to camp. He even saw Ken's dark form creep out of the boathouse, accompanied by the furtive and nervous form of the wiry young fellow from two campsites down. Paulie chuckled, shaking his head. "At least it wasn't two in one weekend," he admitted to himself. He slowly rose and descended the tower, made his way back to the camp, and slipped back into his tent.

He heard Doug startle awake. "Huh? Paulie? Everything okay?" There was concern in the sleepy voice, and Paulie smiled, setting his glasses on top of his shoes.

"Yes, my love," he whispered, snuggling close to his lover's body, feeling the warmth mingle with his own.

Doug came a little bit more awake. "You're hot," he said, softly. "Are you sure you're okay? You're not running a fever, are you?"

Paulie kissed Doug's forehead. "No, dear. It's pretty warm out there, and I was just out for a walk. It's quite a moon out tonight."

Paulie could see Doug's white teeth gleaming in the darkness. "Yeah? Wanna go skinny dipping?"

Paulie chuckled. "That is tempting," he admitted.

The two of them slipped out of the tent and stole, on bare feet, down to the water's edge. Their bodies, made pale by the moonlight, rippled the dark water, causing the silver surface to break into erratic shards. Paulie felt the cool beach sand under his toes, and the cool lake water caressing up his body. Doug, ever at home in the water, ducked under almost at once, and came up nearly silently behind him, hugging him from behind. Paulie chuckled and lay back, letting his beloved's arms encircle him and hold him up. He closed his eyes and let Doug tow him around the shallow water, slowly. The water was over his ears, and he reveled in the darkness, and the silence, and the warmth, as he was slowly tugged around like a child. "I love you," he whispered, the sound of his own voice dulled by the water in his ears. And although he could not hear what the lips that pressed to his had whispered back, he knew.

6 Kinsey Circle

Circles Issue 3

Introduction by Andrew French

Issue Three takes place during the Fall of 2001. The first story, "Paper Faces on Parade," takes its title from the song "Masquerade" from Andrew Lloyd Weber's The Phantom of the Opera and is set at the end of September. The events of 9/11 were still pretty fresh for us, and I added some references to it in the script as I was editing the text.

Folks have asked if the wolf character, Cam, who is Ken's current fella at the beginning of the issue, is a nod to Cameron Wolfe, who has done some great fan art of our characters. The honest answer is, "I don't know." I didn't specifically do that, but I did know Cameron's art, so I may have done so subconsciously to thank him. I'll say so publicly now. Cam, I love the fan art!

We threw our first references to Linda in this issue, a character who is just now appearing in Issue 6. She died in a car crash with a drunk driver just days after 9/11, and I wanted to show that irony. This, of course, has far-reaching consequences, but you'll need to get Issue 6 to find out what they are.

The second part of Issue 3, "Steppin' Out," takes its title from the Joe Jackson song of the same name. It takes place on Halloween 2001.

One of the strongest bits of Issue 3 came about by accident. I had originally called for the image of Taye and Marty kissing to be surrounded by hearts and flowers and with cupid in the upper right corner aiming his bow at them. Scott left the space blank... couldn't make it look good. So I decided to write something to fill that spot. This led to a passage which, I'm led to understand, is being used by at least one minister as something to be read at weddings. Which is, like, wow!

I promise I only call Steve "love wumps" when I'm teasing him.

Dear Douglas,

It's that wonderful time of year again. The leaves have changed colors and are starting to fall off the trees, only to be raked up and tossed into garbage bags. Winter will be here soon. Ken and his current beau, Cam, are enjoying the weather while they can. A friend of mine once said something to the tune of "Fall in New England always feels like something is ending." And it does.

This fall, however, also feels like a beginning. Some terrible people have done something crazy, and the whole world seems poised on the verge of something new. I hope it's something good, because it's brought so much pain, especially to you, love. You lost so many colleagues in the madness, and I can see how it's eating at you.

And then, tragically... ironically... to lose someone close to you to something as plebeian as a drunk driver...

I know you cared for Linda, if not exactly in the way she wanted. I don't know what changes that sadness will bring either.

I can smell fires at night, now, as people are stoking up their wood-burning stoves. Lucky sods. Gas heat is fine, but there's something so romantic and cheery about a fireplace. Ah well, life is full of compromises.

Hallowe'en is fast approaching, and everyone's got their plans. Ken, Taye, and Marty are planning to go to a Halloween Costume Dance that's being held at Paradise Island, now that Joe's reopened the place. It's something of a first date for Marty and Taye, which is so sweet. It makes me think about our "first date," and all the craziness that led up to it. Ah, me. But that's the past, and a story you already know so well.

And then there's poor Arthur. You're really so unfair to him, love, and it seems to be getting worse, rather than better. Something's going to come to a head, and soon. Arthur's good at hiding how upset he gets at the way you treat him, but his mask is slipping...

All our masks are...
Doug, we need to talk.
Circles
Part One: Paper Faces on Parade

No, please. Now.
Maybe later, Arthur? These bags are heavy.

Okay, fine. Talk.

Doug, if this past week has taught me anything, it's how uncertain the future is. I want to put this... pain to rest. I know you blame me for what happened to Paulie. If there were any way to change the past, I would. I wish a hundred times a day that I'd been the one that got sick instead of Paulie.
Yeah, well, that makes two of us.

Douglas, I... yeah, okay... it was my fault we got drunk that night and my fault the kid was here. But I didn't tell Paulie to sleep with him. I mean, Jesus, Paulie doesn't blame me. Why do you?
I can't believe I'm even having this friggin' conversation.

Listen, Doug, I love Paulie. He's like my big brother. I would never have taken him out if I thought it was gonna be trouble. But it happened. Please, can't we find a way to be friends?

Can't we find some way to put this whole thing behind us?

Look, Paulie wanted out of the whole scene, and you dragged him out for "one more night."
If you hadn't pushed him into that, you would've gone out alone, and it'd be you dying instead of him, okay? So forgive me if I can't just "get over that."
I... oh, God, Doug. Don't you think I would die if it meant Paulie would live?

Too bad that you can't, huh? Makes saying things like that easier, though, I bet.

Hey, love, I got some...

Doug, how could you? Those are some of the most hateful things I've ever heard anyone say. Arthur's my oldest friend. I know you blame him, but for the *last* time, it wasn't *his* fault! It was mine! 100% mine! If you can't get that fact through your head, I...
Well, I just don't know what I'll do!

W-where are you going?
To comfort a friend.

I just can't believe some of the things he said. They were so...
I know, dear. I'm very sorry for that. I know I'm not the one you need the apology from, but...
I just... he's never been that direct and venomous before. Usually there would have been a snide comment, a look... maybe ignoring me totally, but this. Oh, man. It hurt so bad.

Well, you know, Douglas lost quite a few of his colleagues in this whole tragedy, and he lost someone he once... cared about a great deal. That might've put everything about me being sick a little higher in his mind. So, maybe you just caught him at exactly the wrong time. Still, that doesn't excuse it.
I just don't get it. I've tried to be friends with him. But doesn't he understand? I didn't want this to happen. I didn't... want...
Arthur, what happened was not your fault. Yes, it was your idea to go out drinking to "mourn" my "retirement". But Keith was my friend first. I'd slept with him before, and I thought to myself, "Why not?"

I know. We've talked about this before. But every time Doug brings it up, it's like a fresh wound.
I know. I will talk to him about it. I'm not going to see my best friend torn apart by this. Doug is going to have to put this behind him... or else... well...
No, Paulie! Don't break up with Doug over this! I'm not worth it.
Well, God knows I don't want to. I love Doug, 12 years now, the picture of a doting husband. But this just sticks my craw so badly. I just want to find a way to end this craziness.

I appreciate that, Paulie. I love you, and I like Doug a lot... well, except when he's like what he was just now.
I know, my dear friend, I know.
Hmmm... painting Marty?

Heh, yeah. He's a pretty good subject, even if he is kind of body shy. Kinda wish I'd been the one advertising for a roommate.
Well, you're so good at getting your subjects to relax.
Hmmm..

What is it?

I just had a thought. Will you paint something for me?

Of course I will! What do you want?
A picture of me and Douglas.
You think he'll sit for me?
Well, lets find out, shall we?

You hurt him badly, you know. I hate it when you treat him like that.
I know. I'm really sorry, Paulie. I should really go and apologize.

It's just... every time I see him, I remember how you got sick, and...

No, you don't.
Beg pardon?
You don't "remember" what happened. You weren't there. You remember my stories.
Okay, right. I remember what you've told me.
Then how is it you never remember that I've told you it wasn't Arthur's fault?

I guess I feel like I can't blame you. You're my perfect guy, after all. Arthur.. Yeah, ok, I know it isn't Arthur's fault. I've been thinking about it a lot. I just get so angry, and then I lash out.
Arthur's just an easy target more often than not.

Do you mean all this, or is it just what you think I want to hear?
Which answer will get me out of this argument quicker?

Okay, truth is I just don't know, Paulie. I still feel a lot of anger, and I do blame Arthur, in part, but I'm willing to try and put it behind us.
When you started going downstairs, I thought you were just going to walk out the door, and I realized I'd gone too far. I was way out of line. I was so scared I was going to lose you, and I... I don't think I could take losing anything else right now. So, yeah, I did some serious thinking.
Think he'd accept an apology, if I went down?

I suspect he might. He's always been a big proponent of forgive and forget.

Well, maybe he can give me a few lessons on that.

I love you, very much, you know.
Well, I don't know what I did to deserve it, but I'm glad.
And it so happens that I love you too...

* KNOCK KNOCK *
Who is it?

It's Doug, Arthur. Can I talk to you?
What about?

I came to apologize. I'm really... really sorry for what I said.
Okay, come on down.

Look, Arthur, those things I said... I'm really sorry. There's a lot going on with me right now, but... I had no right to talk to you that way.
No, you sure didn't.

I know you care about Paulie a lot, and I know it wasn't really your fault... what happened. I'm sorry I've been treating you like that. If you're still willing, I like to try to put the whole thing... well, everything behind us.
I'm willing to give it a shot. You think you can do it?

Yeah, I think I can. And, if there's anything I can do to make up to you for what I said, earlier... well, really... just name it and I'll do it.
Well, no. I don't want to put it on those terms.
But there is something...

Sure. Ask.
Well, you know that portrait I did of Paulie, way back when? I've wanted to do a more modern follow up. But...
I can't imagine painting Paulie without you. If Paulie's ok with it, would you pose for me?

You want to paint me? And Paulie? Together?
Yes. Exactly. A nude, with the two of you embracing.
Nude? Um...
Don't tell me that you're shy?
Maybe a little. I usually don't get naked in front of.. well....
What?
Heh. I was going to say "strangers." We're still sort of strangers to each other. My fault.

Hey, forgive and forget, remember?
Hello. I'm Arthur Korsky.

Douglas Pope. A pleasure to meet you.
Likewise. And now, we're not strangers. So, will you pose for me, if Paulie agrees?
If Paulie agrees... oh, sure, why not? If Marty and Ken can do it, I can do it.

Cool. I'll have to get some more paint, but we can start tomorrow evening, if you guys are willing.
You know... I really am sorry. We could have been good friends by now, if I hadn't...

Forgive and forget, Doug. No regrets. There's still plenty of time to be friends, right?
Right. So let's go ask Paulie.

Dear Douglas,
I'm pleased to see that tensions are being eased off between you & Arthur. As time goes by, I think you're both going to find that you have a lot in common, & I think a good friendship can grow.

If you can keep doing what you're doing, that is. What are you doing, you ask?
Well, prior to this fight, you were both keeping civil masks on around each other. Then, on the stairway, you dropped that mask, but the face you showed there was a mask too. Behind the anger you were showing him, you were hiding fear, which I know you hate showing to anyone.
I wish I could take that fear away and tell you I'll never leave you. but we both know I just can't promise you that. I can't give you "always."

I can only give you "as long as I can." And that's just another mask you and I both wear, pretending it doesn't bother either of us.
For now, anyway, you and Arthur have taken off your masks. I must applaud you both for that, and I hope that you keep them off for good.
I hope you know that, no matter what happens, I will love you always.
Love,
Paulie

One month later ...

Dear Douglas,

Well, the big night is here. Samhain. All Hallow's Eve.

Call it what you will, it's Hallowe'en.

Part Two: Steppin' Out

Our neighborhood gremlins are arriving in droves. Probably because they know from experience that Taye insists we spring for full-sized candy bars, rather than snack packs. Thank God for Costco ...

Hallowe'en has always been a favorite of mine. I love seeing all the decorations, the costumes, and the silly, scary movies on T.V. And, your pumpkin soup recipe is to die for!

Tonight's also a big night for Taye & Marty. who are going on the official "first date." They and Ken are going to boogie the night away... or whatever "boogie" has been replaced with now.

You know who just "dropped by?" Carter Allen. Would you believe he won't even let his kids trick-or-treat here? Man! Sometimes I think he's trying to piss me off..
Probably thinks we're injecting our Snickers bars with special chemicals that turn kids gay, or something.
Still, what can you do? Some folks just don't like us. If he's that much of a butt-head, who wants him around, frankly?

I know. But who needs that crap? And, he's poisoning his kids against us. They're gonna grow up thinking gays are evil, sex-crazed perverts that hump anything that moves.

Hey, how do I look? Does this make me look hot? Think I'll score tonight?

What? Why are you guys smirking? Do I look stupid?
Oh... heh... no, Ken. We were just amused by the universe's sense of timing.

Well, now...this is certainly a jovial scene. What's happening down here?
I dunno; I just got here. Personally, I think Arthur spiked the punch.
I think you have to be doing it secretively in order to be accused of "spiking" it.

Hiya.
Hi Marty. You look good. Ready for the big dance?

I guess so. I'm not much of a dancer.
Heh, you and me both. But Paulie & John still used to drag me out. Just think of it as an adventure.

Adventure. Excitement. A Jedi craves not these things.
How about a Snickers?
Um... that we crave.

You look wonderful, dear. Very much like a real Jedi.
Plus a few pounds.
Judge me not by my size.

Well, your Jedi-ness, is your date ready yet?
Well, he wouldn't put on his costume until I left the bedroom.
It shouldn't take long.

Yoo-hoo!
Angel First-Class Taylor Dooley, reporting for duty.

Wow... You look great, Taye.
Thank you, Master Jedi.

We should probably get going. The T is gonna be crowded tonight.
Have fun, children. Don't do anything we wouldn't do.
Sure you don't wanna come?

Not tonight, dear. We're going to finish up giving out candy, and then Douglas & I are sitting for Arthur again.

Oh, yeah! The painting! How's that going, Arthur?
Well, I don't want to jinx it, but... it's a masterpiece!
Hmph! He won't even let us see it!

This is gonna be great. After the last couple of months, we all deserve a good party. Ready, Marty?
Oh, as ready as I'll ever be, I expect.

So... explain again why we shouldn't be worried that I'm not 21 yet?
Because we know people!

Look, this club is 18 years and up. If you're underage, you just wear a wristband and they won't let you buy drinks. The owner, Joe, had an 18-year old boyfriend when they opened, so he arranged it like that.
Oh... okay... that does make sense.

Heh... you should tell him who the 18-year old was!
?
Oh, shut up, Ken.

We're here!
PARADISE
Wow!

Hey, handsome.
Yo, Marc.

Well, hey, Taye. Who's your friend?
This is Marty, my new... roommate. Marty, this is Marc. He's a doorman here.

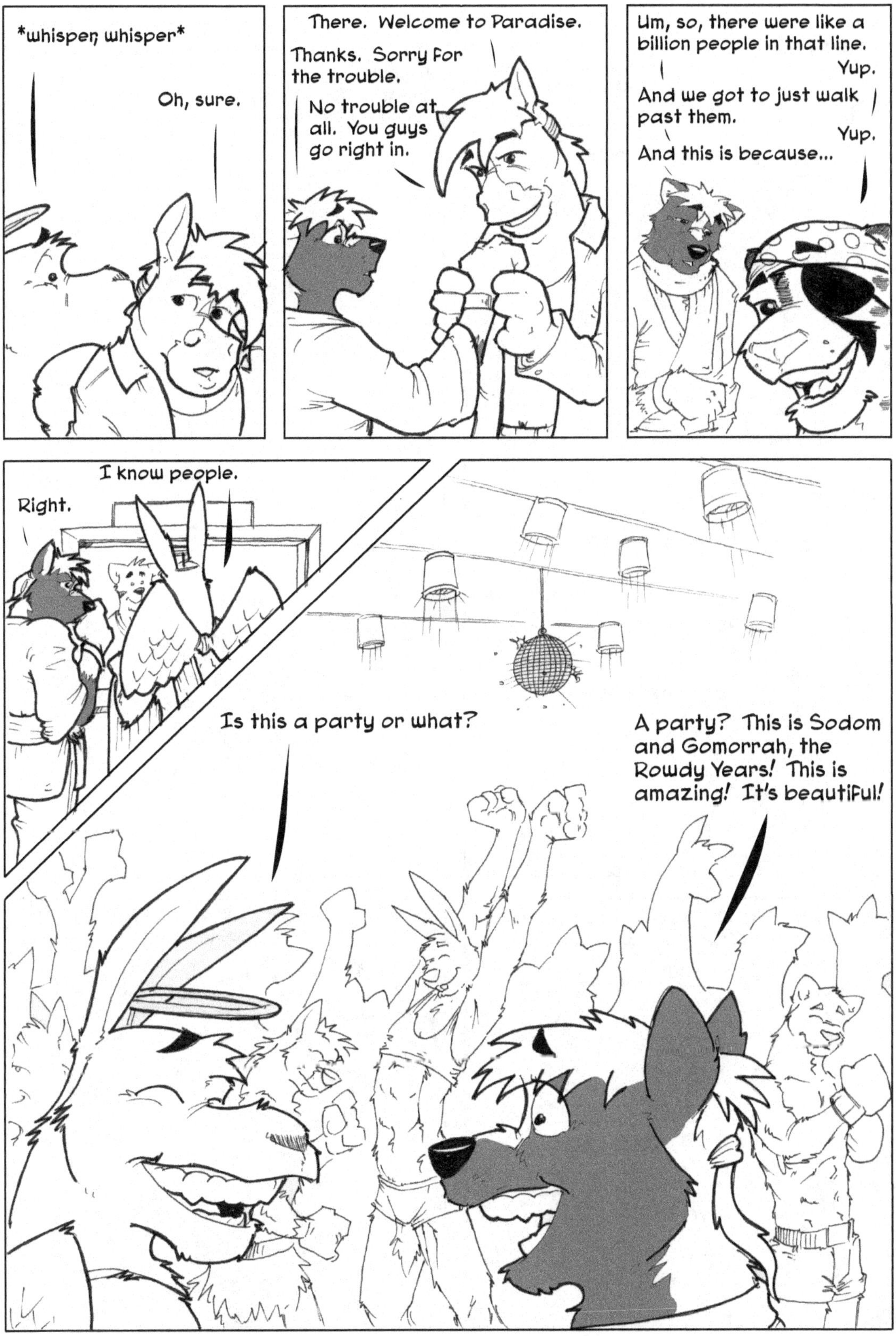

I know people.

Right.

Is this a party or what?

A party? This is Sodom and Gomorrah, the Rowdy Years! This is amazing! It's beautiful!

Knew you'd like it! There's a couple of folks you've got to meet.
Well, I've got to catch up with somebody. I'll see you guys later!
Have fun, Ken!

Stick with me, kiddo! Such sights I have to show you...
Don't let go of me, please. I'm feeling a little overwhelmed.
What?!

I said, I'm feeling overwhelmed!
Perfectly understandable!

Wow! Ken's fast, huh?
What do you mean?
He's already talking to someone.

Yup! He's fast! Oh, I see Jesús over there! You've got to meet him!
Hello, Taye!

Roger? What the fuck are you doing here?
It's a free country, isn't it?

What do you want, Roger?
Heard you were here! Wanted to say hi! So, who's this?
Hi! I'm Marty, Taye's roommate!

Get lost, Roger! We have nothing to say to each other!
This is your new roommate? Should I be offended or amused?
You should be going, Asshole! C'mon, Marty!

I'm sorry, Marty! That was Roger, my ex-boyfriend!
Easy to see what I saw in him, huh?

Well... it's easier to see what he saw in you.
You charmer! C'mon. Let's dance!

pant, pant Oh, my God! I can't believe how out of shape I am!
Looked good to me, my brave Jedi knight!
Oh! There's Jesús! Quick! This way!

He's so wonderful! You've got to meet him. Jesús! Jesús!

Taye, querido! It's so good to see you! And this must be Marty, no?
It's a pleasure to meet you.

Oh, Chica! I like this one! Where can I get one?
Can't have this one! He's Mine!

You selfish bitch! Well, can I at least borrow him?
Only til I get back with some drinks.

That's a really awesome costume, Jesús!
Costume? No, no, hermoso! This mask is my costume!

Oh! Gee, I've never met a...um...
Choose your words carefully, Hermoso!
Um...drag queen?
Good choice of words. You may live.

I've just never met one before.
Heh. You're sweet, Marty. Much nicer than some guys my friends have dated.
Thanks. At least I've gotta be better than that Roger guy of Taye's, huh?
Oh, you think so, you fat fucker?

Roger!!
Roger, chico, don't you do anything stupid! You know Joe won't stand for any fighting in here!
Who's fighting? Why don't you just stay out of this, Jesús? This has nothing to do with you!
It's cool, Jesús! Nothing's gonna happen, right, Roger?

I can't believe he threw me out for you!
What? What're you talking about?
I'm out of the picture, and he brings you in! Tell me, did you two fuck the first night after I was gone, or what?
Dude, you're not making sense!
Playing stupid, eh? Think I'll care? I'll tear you apart, you little shit!

I don't think so, asshole!
What the fuck do you think you're doing Roger?

Stay out of it, Taye! I'm gonna flatten this little cupcake!

SWISH!

SMACK!

I broke up with you, asshole, because of shit like this! You stupid bully!
I'm warning you, Roger! Stay away from me and my friends!

What the *HELL* is goin' on over here?
He started it!

Taye... Jeez, man! What did you do that for? You know I'm gonna have to ask ya t'leave!
Oh, come on, Marc! Taye may have landed the first punch, but he didn't throw the first!
That's okay, Jesús... we'll go, Marc. I've had enough partying for one night.
Yeah... I'm good.

I'm just gonna get some ice for my hand, okay?
Sure. Just ask at the bar.
C'mon, handsome. We'll get the coats.

That fucking slut! I should...
You should go home and sober up!
Oh, and by the way, you can stay out of our club for a while! If I see you around here, especially on a night Taye shows up, I'll bounce your ass!

Sorry you have to go so early, chica.

We'll come back on a less crazy night, I promise.

You'd better, hermana. And you call me soon, okay? And Marty? It's been a real pleasure.

Likewise, Jesús.

Sheesh. One slap and I sprain my wrist. Am I a wuss or what?

Well, you didn't look too wussy when you were decking that jerk.
Well, I had to defend the honor of my snuggly guy, didn't I?
I guess.

Hey! What's wrong?
Well, I've got all these questions, now...
Such as?
Well... for starters, who was the 18-year old? You know... the club-owner's boyfriend? You hushed Ken up about it...

Hee! You thought that was me?
Well... you are the guy who "knows people."
Well, yeah. I make friends easily. I didn't mean in the biblical sense.
Well, who was it, then?
It was Ken. Joe was his first boyfriend.

Well... okay... can I sum up the rest of my worries in two questions?
Sure.
Of the people we met tonight, how many have you slept with?
One. Roger.
Only Roger?

Prior to him, there was only a very sweet guy in New York named Chris, and that ended when I moved to Boston.
I'm a very flirtatious guy, Marty, but that doesn't mean I want to sleep with everyone I meet.

Okay, second question. What are we to each other? Tonight, you were introducing me as your roommate...

Oh, I'm not wild about labels, hon, but if you like, I'll call you my boyfriend. I mean, we can't use "lover" or "partner" yet, technically... and "significant other" sounds like something you check on a form...
Partner sounds like we're going into business together..

Actually, I really like it when you call me Teddy Bear.
Mmmmm... I like calling you that, too. Could be much worse. Chris used to call me Love Wumps.
And... ummm... I was thinking... this is our first date...

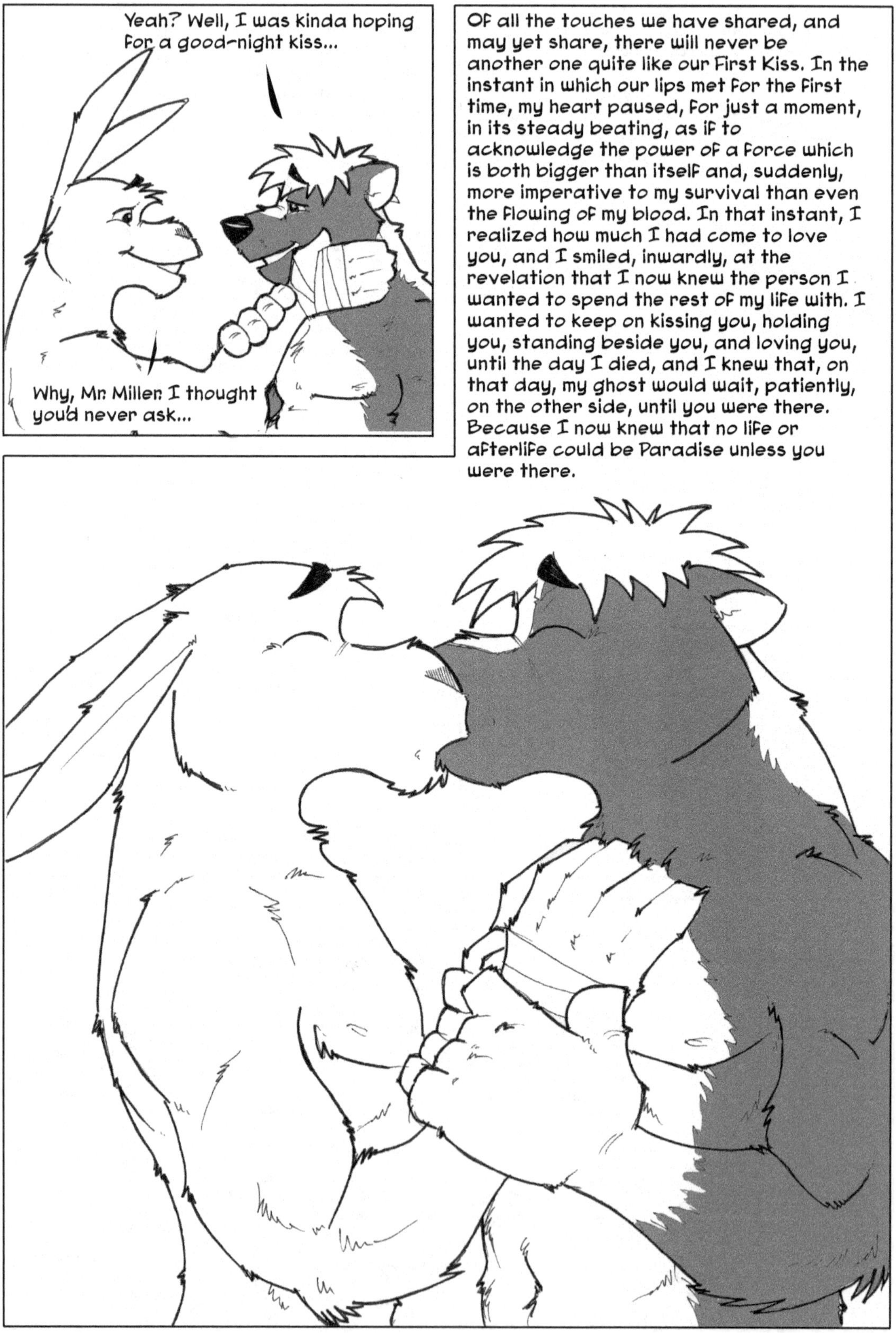

Of all the touches we have shared, and may yet share, there will never be another one quite like our First Kiss. In the instant in which our lips met for the first time, my heart paused, for just a moment, in its steady beating, as if to acknowledge the power of a force which is both bigger than itself and, suddenly, more imperative to my survival than even the flowing of my blood. In that instant, I realized how much I had come to love you, and I smiled, inwardly, at the revelation that I now knew the person I wanted to spend the rest of my life with. I wanted to keep on kissing you, holding you, standing beside you, and loving you, until the day I died, and I knew that, on that day, my ghost would wait, patiently, on the other side, until you were there. Because I now knew that no life or afterlife could be Paradise unless you were there.

sigh That was pretty nice.
That was worth the wait!
Want to do some more?
You're ready for more?

I meant more kissing.
Oh... heh... sorry.

There's no rush, Marty. When you're ready, I'll be here. I'd rather take it slow and go all the way when you're ready.
Til then, we can practice our kissing.

Thanks, Taye. I'm still a little leery, but... I think about it a lot.
When we do it, it'll be my first time for a lot of stuff. I'm glad it'll be with you.

Love wumps.
Hee!

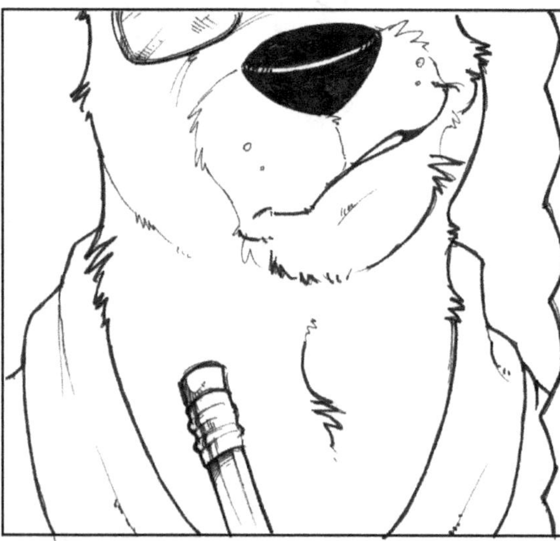

Dear Douglas,

The night for masks ends.
Costumes are stored 'til next year.
We still have candy.

That was my Hallowe'en haiku.

I just got in from my gardening, but I didn't get much done. Someone had festooned our yard with toilet paper, so I spent most of the morning cleaning it up.

The trouble is, I have to wonder if they did it as a simple prank, or if we were singled out because we're gay. I hate having to wonder about things like that.

I gather that Mary and Taye had an eventful evening last night from what Marty told me before heading off to school. From the fact that Ken hasn't come home yet, I'd say the same is true of him.

And, as if I needed this, just as I'm getting things between you and Arthur somewhat settled, it would seem that Ken is up to something regarding Marty and Taye. I hope that can be settled amicably, and soon.

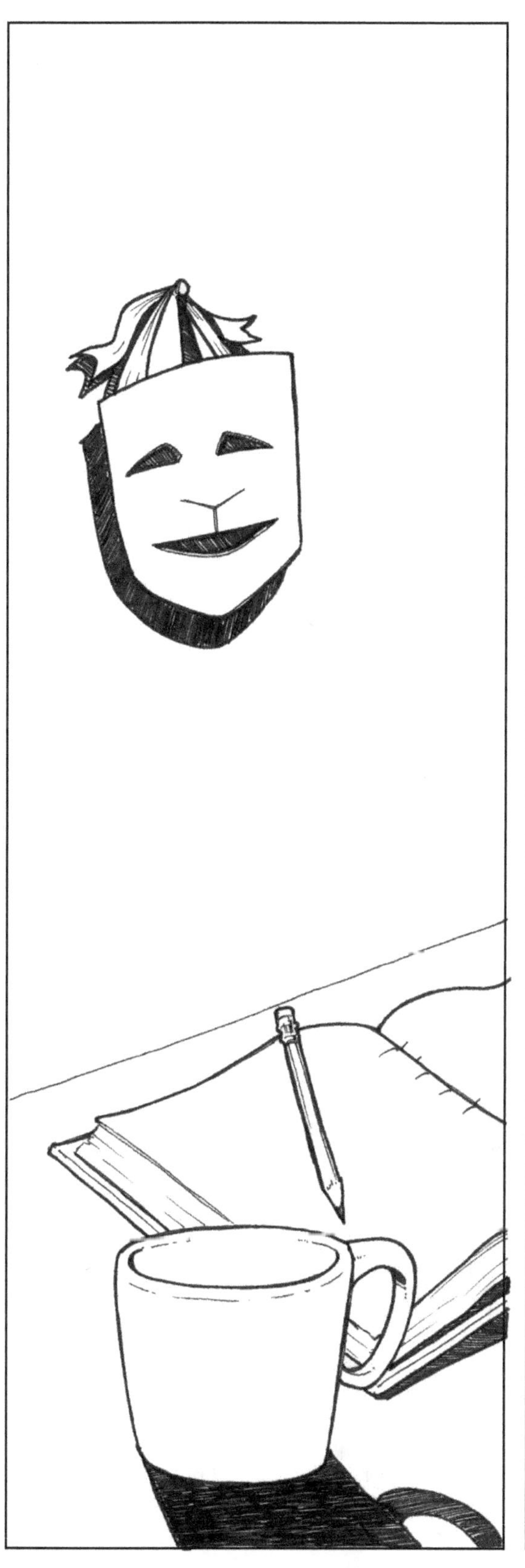

I'm really getting too old for this sort of thing. Really.

All in all, though, these last couple of weeks have made me think about things. About how people use and wear masks.

Some people, like Marty, have none. The Marty I see inside is the same Marty I see on the surface.

Ken, on the other hand... I feel like there are depths to Ken that he won't let any of us see.

On the other hand, who am I to talk? The only way I can get through a day, sometimes, is to put on my happy mask and joke my way towards my final days.

I hope this isn't too depressing for you, my love. Please believe me when I say you make those days rare indeed for me.

Anyway, closing for now. There is always so much to be doing around here. Idle rich, indeed.

Love,
Paulie

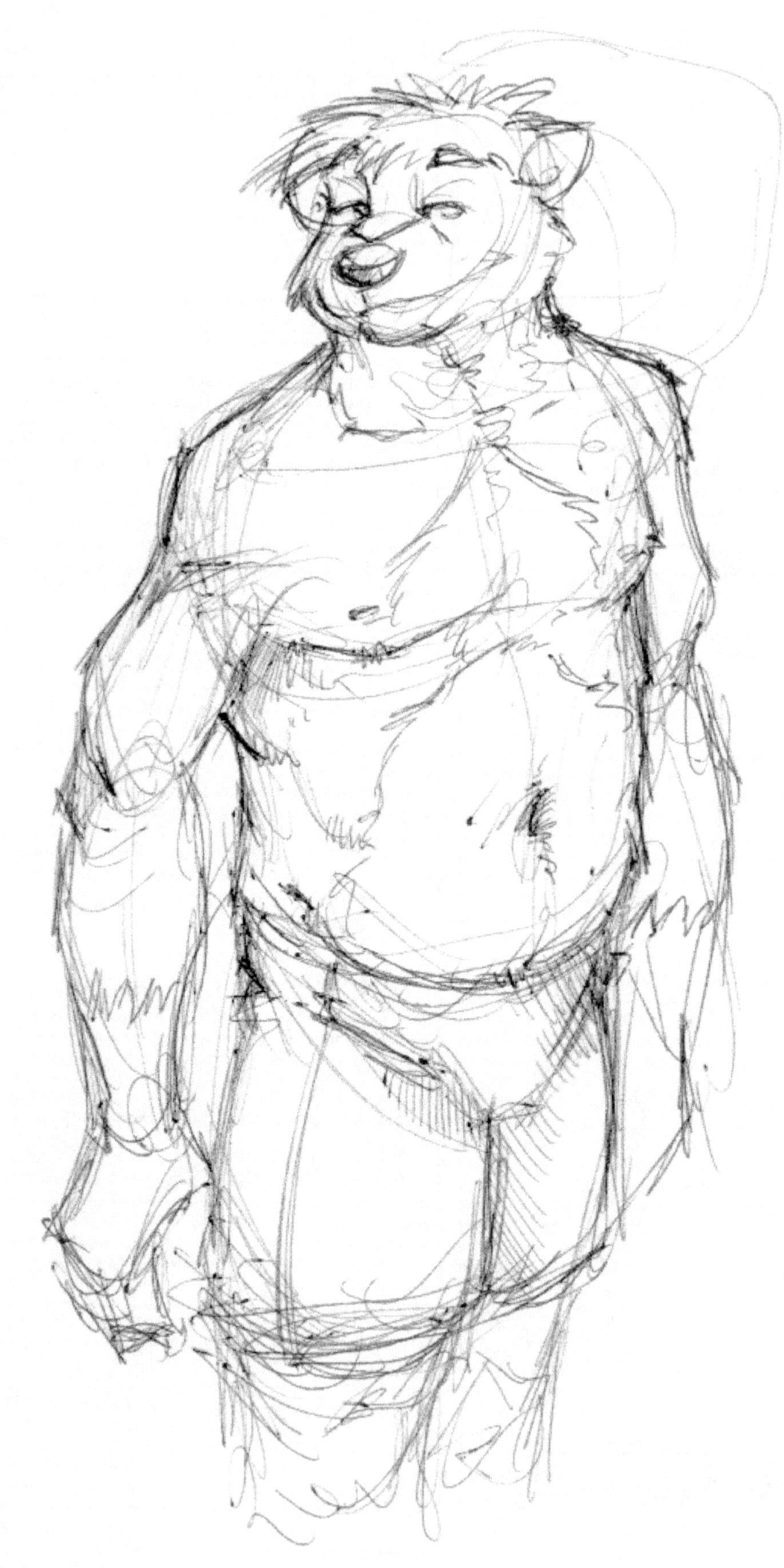

Circles Issue 4

Introduction by Andrew French

Issue 4, "In His Anger and His Shame," takes its title from "The Boxer" by Simon & Garfunkel. It is set around Christmas 2001.

Yes, I am that spastic around Christmas... both as Paulie and Douglas.

And we finally got around to getting John back into the picture. There's lots more of him coming in Issues 7 and beyond, I promise. I know folks like him. And, while Michael Lang was originally intended to be a one-shot character, Scott's design of him was so appealing that he's become a more important character in the book.

Dave is based strongly on my buddy Randy Milholland. He's named for the character Davan from Randy's comic strip, Something Positive. His line "Bite me, you rug-munching sasquatch," actually took the most work in this issue. I tried over and over again to find just the right insult, and I think that nailed it pretty hard.

I think this issue redeems a lot of Ken's negative qualities, as well as shows that Marty has some balls on him. And the boxing scene, which Scott added on his own (my script cut from "Let's dance, asshole," to them carrying Mac away) is some great stuff.

As to what happens after Marty and Taye sink out of scene... that's my homage to a scene in Elfquest, one of my favorite indy comics.

The shirt Taye's wearing is, of course, the peach-colored shirt mentioned in Issue 2. And the tie Paulie has given Doug in the Christmas scene most likely has baby ducks on it, a la Issue 1.

Dear Douglas,
Ho, ho, ho!!!

Yes, yes, I know. I should write something about the crass commercialism of Christmas here, or how it was usurped from ancient Pagan traditions, or something similarly harsh to show what a witty and urbane and cynical person the world has made me...

YULE
Hmmm...

You and I both know, however, that if I tried to say that I don't care for Christmas, it would be a blatant lie.

I LOVE Christmas. I'm a junkie for it. I crave it every year like a drowning man craves air. I spend all autumn straining towards it in my soul. Maybe it's my way of keeping young... or at least immature.
But I'm sure that I shall always love Christmas.

Do you mind? This is private.
But I saw my name on that page. It caught my eye.
Your name is on EVERY page. I could hardly keep a journal otherwise.

Well, then, you can't blame me for being curious! I wanna read it!
I've told you. Later.

Ah! But it IS later. I checked the clock.
Patience, dear heart. You can read it when the time is right.
I hate being patient.

Why don't you go offer to help Arthur? You can ask him about the party.
Hmph. A painfully transparent attempt to distract me from my rightful reading material.

Will you go help Arthur, you silly thing?
Yeah, yeah...

You get pretty excited around Christmas, yourself, like a kid who wants to peek at his presents. But by making up with Arthur...
...you've already given me what I wanted for Christmas...

Peace on Earth...

or at least in our little corner of it.
Heya, Art! Need any help with those lights?
Circles
In His Anger and His Shame

Hey, sure, Doug. Got one more section to do, and then we'll be finished.
Y'know, it never ceases to amaze me.
What's that?

How ga-ga Paulie goes at Christmas.
I mean, he doesn't go to church or anything.

He's always been that way, too. I think he uses Christmas as his way of celebrating another year with his "Family."

Does it seem to you he's really added to the lights lately?

That IS more recent. Somehow, I suspect it's his way of thumbing his nose at Carter Allen.
Well, we both know the dignified Mr. Mayhew could never publicly go after that self-righteous dickhead. I guess I could see this as suburban warfare... out Christmasing the straight folks...

Speaking of suburban warfare... shall we launch the first volley?
You may fire at will, Sir.

Jingle Bells, Jingle Bells,
Jingle all the way!
...mumble, mumble...

FWAASH!!!
Gah!!!

Wow!
Lookit, Daddy!

S'even better'n last year!
Yeah!

SLAM

That's my Paulie.

Wow... that is really... gaudy.
Yes. Yes it is.

Heh. Don't let Paulie hear you say that, though. He loves those lights.
No, no. I mean it in a good way. Thanks for doing it, by the way.

Of course. Paulie knows I'd do anything for him.
Well, you put up with me all that time.

Don't you bring that up. It's over. Everything's cool between us.
Yeah... well... that's kind of the other reason I'm down here.

Oh? Well, what's up, Doug?
Well, you know that family shelter I've gotten my work involved with?

Sure. That's actually one the things I always admired about you. You get so involved and passionate with these community projects and stuff...
Yeah? Well, um... how'd you like to get involved?

Sure! I'd be happy to. You need a building painted or something?
Um... well, no. It's a little more... It's different than that.

Okay... spit it out. What do you need?

Well, we're having a Christmas party in a couple of weeks. The kids sent letters to Santa with lists of stuff they want, and we wanted to have Santa hand them out to the younger kids.

Aw... that's really cute. You need me to pick up some stuff? I'd be glad to make a donation.
Um... actually... I was kind of hoping you'd... hand the gifts out?

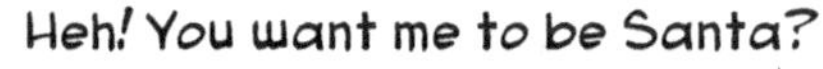
Heh! You want me to be Santa?

One guy was gonna do it, only now his kid is getting married, and no one else is the right size and build for it...
Sure. I'll do it.
Really?

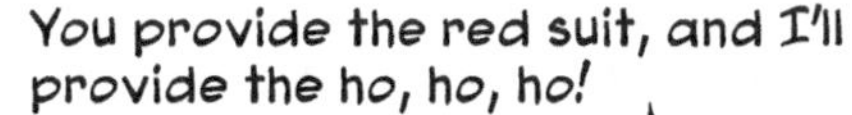
You provide the red suit, and I'll provide the ho, ho, ho!

Oh, man, Art. You're a saint!

After all, it's Christmas. And what else are friends for?

The tree looks really pretty. Never had a real one before. I mean, we had a fake one in my dorm...

Of course, it kind of tended to get decorated with ornaments made out of beer cans and stuff.
Well, alcohol says Christmas to a lot of people.
Well, this is way nicer anyhow. Smells great, too.

My family always got a real tree. My holiday wouldn't be complete without that smell.

I can't wait to put presents under it!
Well, celebrating Hanukkah with your folks was fun, too! It's neat having presents every day.

Well, you can tell my folks are really taking to the idea of us being together. You got better presents than me.
I can't help it if I inspire people's generous natures.

Which reminds me... what was the Hanukkah gift that Ken gave you?
A free trial at his gym. I kinda get the feeling Ken is teasing me.

I'm not sure Ken is that subtle. He may think he's doing you a favor.
I'm thinking of redeeming it.

Really?! Why?
Well... I know you don't mind me like this...

I LOVE you like this.
Yeah... but I've put on some pounds since Thanksgiving. I was thinking of trying to lose 'em.

Well, it's up to you. I don't mind the extra pounds, hon. Really.
I know.
clink

Well, hey there, stranger.
Yo, Johnny. Long time no see.

And to what do I owe the honor?
Christmas shopping. Gotta find sumpin' for Taye.

Well, I woulda recommended that new Broadway collection, but Marty already picked that up for him.
Marty, huh? Well, that figures.

They've really become quite the item, huh?
Mm... I guess.

Well, never saw that before.
Saw what?
You jealous.

Jealous? Jealous of who?
Marty. Never realized you were that hot for Taye. Not that I blame you.

Marty? Pft. That'll be the day. I mean, Taye's hot and all, but jealous of Marty? That's ridiculous.
Why? Just cause Marty's chubby? He mentioned the coupon for the gym you gave him...

He's more than just chubby. Anyway this is stupid. I'm not jealous of Marty. I gave him that as a Hanukkah present.
And that has nothing to do with making him look bad in front of your gym pals?

This is so dumb. It's just a gift. I'm trying to be nice... help him out.
Well, whatever. Not my business I guess.

Hey... you're Ken Brassai, aren't
Yeah, so?

I'm Michael Lang. You went out with my roommate, Darryl, for a few weeks about this time last year.
Mm. Darryl... yeah. You still live with him?

Nope. Got my own place, now. Takin' some graduate classes, workin' at a camera store. How 'bout you?
I dunno. Workin'... Partyin'.

Heh. Just like when you were seein' Darryl. Who you seein' now?
No one, really. You?
No one, really. Say, you busy?

Huh. Jus' some shopping. Whatcha got in mind?
Oh, I'm pretty negotiable, sexy.
Yeah?

Yup. And my place is nearby... it's over this nice little Italian place...
Oh, yeah... I think I know the one.

Guess he'll never change.

HO, HO, HO!
Merry Christmas!
SANTA!
Don't push, now. Santa has time and presents enough for all of you.
And what's your name, little boy?
Jay-Jay!
Have you been a good boy this year, Jay-Jay?
Yessir, Mr. Santa!
Well, I got your letter, Jay-Jay, and I know you asked for something special...
Oh! Oh Wow! Thank you, Mr. Santa! Lookit Dad!

Art, I can't thank you enough, really. It meant so much to the children.
Seriously, Kathy, don't mention it. I had a lot of fun.

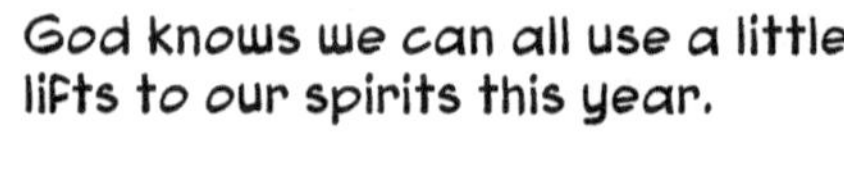
God knows we can all use a little lifts to our spirits this year.

That's sure the truth.
smeck

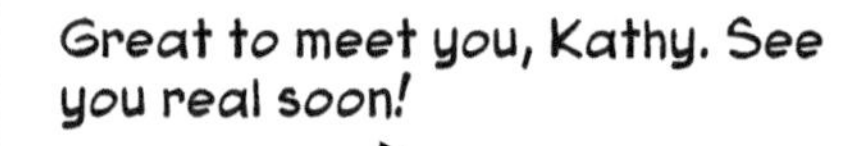
Great to meet you, Kathy. See you real soon!

You and me. Paulie. Christmas. Some family members I've been neglecting. I think I need to do some major house cleaning. Take some responsibility for what I've done in my life instead of running from it.

Well, you're off to a good start, right? We're talking... getting friendly, even.

LOCKER ROOM
I must be crazy...

Hey, Marty! You came!
Well, sure...

HEY, EVERYONE! THIS IS MARTY! HE'S NEW HERE!
Ehhh... Ken. I'm feeling self-conscious as it is...

Huh? Why?
Um... well it's kind of obvious I don't belong here...

Nahh... no one cares. C'mon, man. It's cool. You've taken the first step towards bettering yourself. People respect that. C'mon over and meet my workout partners.
Oy.

Oh, great. Another queer. That's all this place needs...

Okay, big guy. Get it up for me.
ack...

Do you have... oof... any idea how disheartening it is to have a woman say that when you have no chance with her?

Heya, Kenny.
erf... New flame, Ken?

Ha, ha, Dave.
You're Marty, right? You live under Ken? That must be noisy.

Some nights.
Wise-ass.
Heh. I'm Dave. 'S nice t' meetcha.

Hey, there, Marty-boy. Name's Gus. Any friend of Ken's...
Hunh! Uh... likewise...
crunch

So, what're we up to today? You still tryin' to build up those scrawny twigs of yours, Dave?
oy...

More or less. Gus has been happily inflicting her systematic torture on me since I arrived...
snicker
And, how many guys can say they've been worked over by a sadistic lesbian without having to pay her?

Just for that, shrimp, I'm gonna getcha in the sparring ring.
ulp
W-well, when I say sadistic lesbian, I mean it as a friend.

Looks like the peanut gallery's behaving today.
Other than the usual sniggering.
What's up?

Oh, just this one guy, Mac, and his cronies. They have quite a chip on their shoulders about us homos coming in and ruining "their" gym.
Oh, swell.

Assholes like that give us straight guys a bad name.
Dave... you are such a closet case. No one buys that you're straight.
That's just because my last girlfriend went lezbo after sleeping with me.

Thanks for that, by the way. She's a hottie...
Bite me, you rug-munching sasquatch.
That's right, baby. You know I love it when you talk dirty...

Are they always like that?
More or less. Don't worry about them, or about Mac. Let's get you sweatin'!

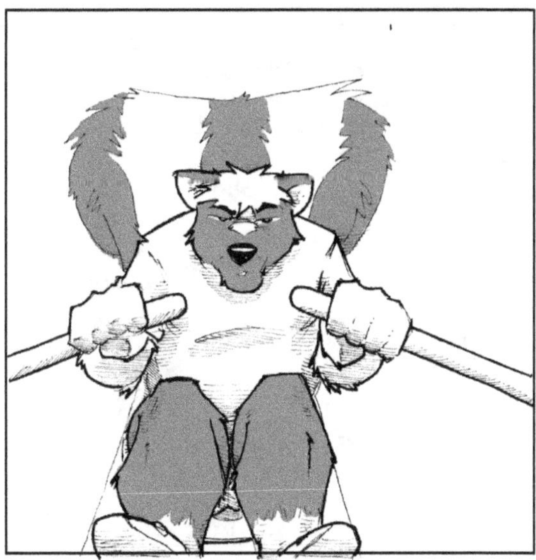

Here... this sports stuff tastes like crap, but it does help you get rehydrated.
Thanks. I don't know the last time I ached this much. I can't believe Ken and Gus are still up and frisky.

Heh. Yeah, they really go at it, don't they? I don't even try to keep up with them any more.

How'd you hook up with them, anyway?
Well, gyms are usually very cliquish. I didn't really fit in with any of the other cliques. These two were both really nice to me.

I'm just trying to buff up a little. I'm not as hardcore as they are.
I doubt anyone's as hardcore as Gus. What's her story?
Well, her real name's Augusta. Don't let the way we talk fool ya. She's really nice. Just hides it well.

She's been picked on since she was a kid, 'cause she's so big. One day, she just decided that, if anyone was gonna give her crap, they were gonna get a Grade-A Ass-Kick.
She looks like she could give one, too.
Got that right. Whoops. Looks like it's my turn in the ring. Have fun.

Hey, Marty. Mind if I have a swig of that?
Huh? Oh... sure.

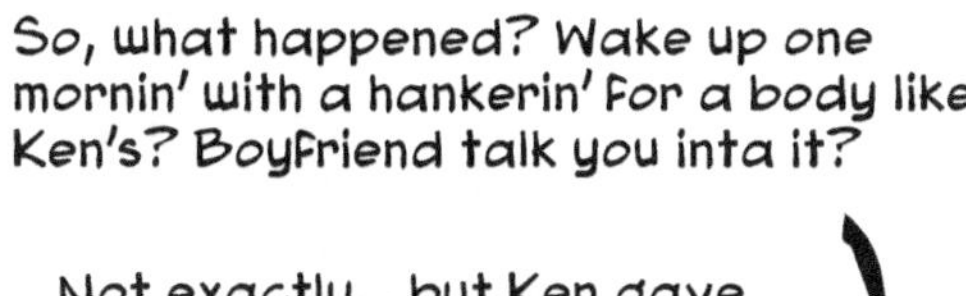
So, what happened? Wake up one mornin' with a hankerin' for a body like Ken's? Boyfriend talk you inta it?

Not exactly... but Ken gave me a free pass, and I didn't want to seem ungrateful...

Well, that's refreshing. So many folks seem to feel the need to be body beautiful. But, really, you're the one who should decide how you need to be.
You wanna work on your bod, then you should go for it, but, if not, who cares what anyone else thinks, even a boyfriend.

Actually, my boyfriend seems to think I'm pretty cute like this. But taking a few pounds off for my health can't be a bad thing, right?
Ever tried boxing? Burns a lot of calories...

Um... I'm kind of averse to getting punched?
Nahh... we'll have ya smack a bag around. They don't hit back... well... not hard, anyway.

Great White Hopeless.
snort

huff
THUD!

Wow... he's still giving it some good smacks. He's got a lot of endurance.
whump
Yeah...

He's tough. I like him.
He's lasting a lot longer than I did on MY first day.

I gotta admit, I didn't think he had it in him. He's impressing the Hell out of me.
You set him up, didn't you? Expected him to back out or wimp out?

I honestly didn't think of it at the time... maybe subconsciously I did.
I guess John was right...

shump

First visit, right? What's yer name?
Uh... Marty.

Well, Marty, since you're new here, I guess I can cut you some slack.
But I'm planning on using this bag, now.
That so?

Hmmmm...

Looks like there's two empty bags over there.

So why don't you go use one?
Why don't you? I don't see why *I* should move.
Oh you don't, huh, queer-boy? We've been pretty tolerant of your friends, so far, but don't push it.

I'm pushing it?! ME? You guys come over and hassle me, and I'M pushing it? Where the Hell do you get off?
Don't you fuckin' shout at me, faggot, or else...
Or else what? You and your friends jump me on the street? Three or four against one? Oooo... big man.

You think I won't take you on, one on one?
You saying you will? So fine. Let's go.
We've got the gloves on. Let's take care of this right here and now. In the ring.

In... the ring?
Ha!
Heh, heh, heh.

What's so damned funny?
Nothin', faggot. Not gonna be nothin' funny about this. Gonna be a goddamned tragedy...
Kill him, Mac!

What's this? A party? And I'm not invited?
Keep out of this, Brassai!
Yeah, Ken. I don't need anyone to protect me.

Believe me, I can see that, Marty. But this is more than them just shovin' you around. They been dickin' around with us since day one. Just 'cause now they think they can beat one of us...
Hmph.

Oh, fuck that noise. I could beat any of you faggots in the ring.
Well, care to back that claim, Mac? We put up one of ours, and you put up one of yours...
Whoever loses has to find another gym.

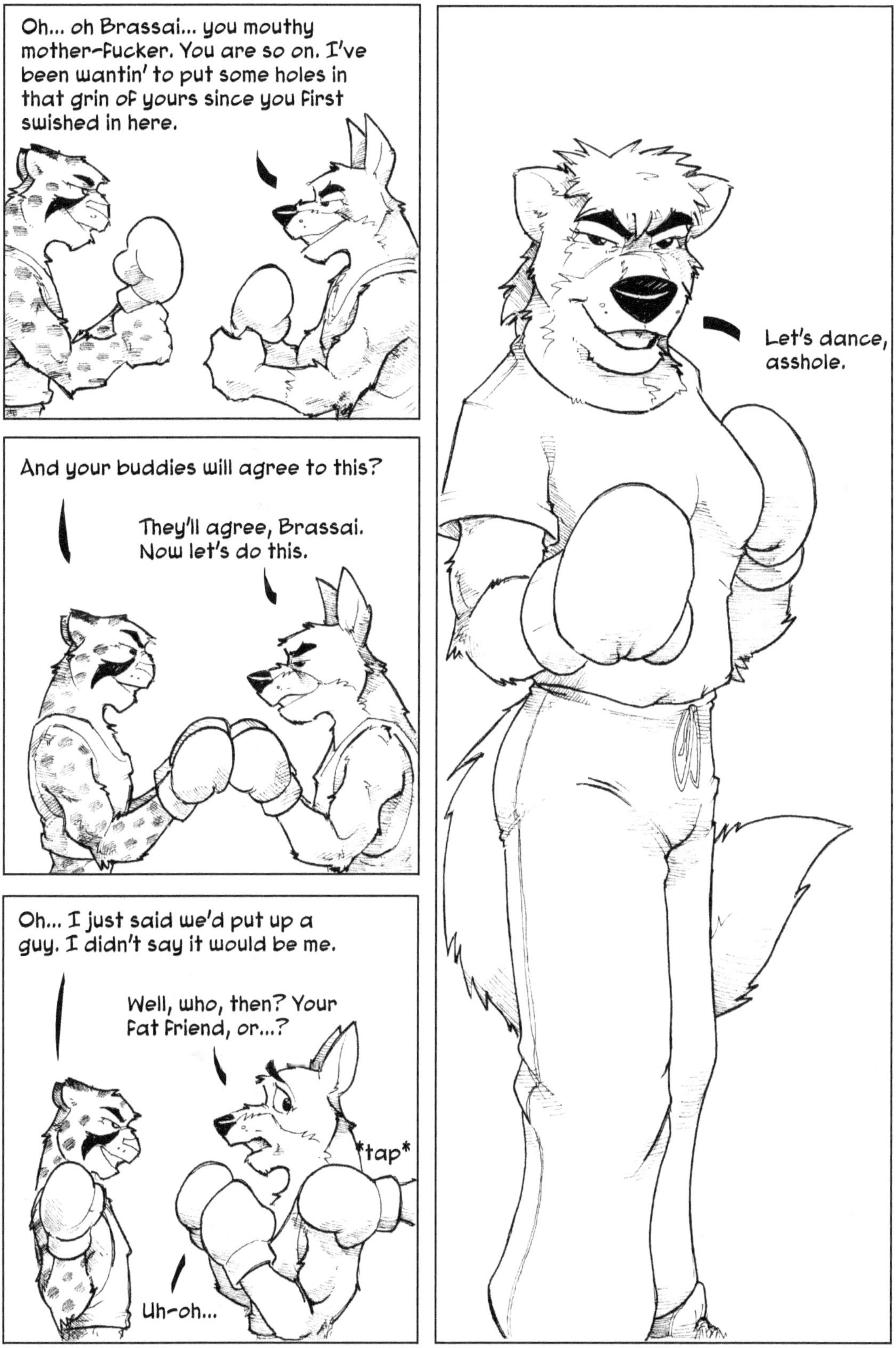

Let's dance, asshole.

WHUMP!!!
OOF!!!
THWOCK!
Unghh... Mama?

Buh-bye! So long!

I had no idea boxing was such a satisfying sport to watch.
Heh... thanks for bein' a great cheerin' section.

I liked the part when you hit him so hard that he started to cry!
Way to go, Champ.
Heh. Thanks
bump

I guess it's naive to hope that they were the only homophobes here?
Nah... they were always just the most vocal about it.

Bet th' others won't bug us for a while, at least, though.
Well, kids. It's been a day, but I have a cat to feed.

Oh, shit, yeah. I gotta get home. Lucy'll kill me if I'm late for dinner.
How can YOU be scared of someone so small?

You haven't been THAT bad. But... I don't understand why you were acting like that, anyway.

Would you believe I was jealous of you and Taye? I've always had a thing for him, and I couldn't figure out why you got him and I didn't.

But you really impressed me today. You worked hard, and you didn't back down. Maybe Taye's just a better judge of folks than me. So... I'm sorry... for everything.
Jealous? Of me?

I was, but now I'm just proud to be your friend. If we can still be friends?
We ARE friends, Ken. I can take a little teasing.

So... you think you re gonna come back to the gym?
Well, I wouldn't say "Never," but it's not really my thing.
Well... y'know, that's cool, too. You're a really good guy, Marty...

Even if you are a little chubby...
Boxing ring's right over there, skinny-boy. Anytime you're feelin' lucky.
Heh, heh, heh.

Lucy! I m home!
Oh, Ricky! Waahh!

So how'd it go, Teddy Bear? I missed ya!
It went really well. Not sure I'd go on a regular basis, but it was fun.
Cool.

You're not all sweaty and stinky, are you?
No. I showered.

Mmmm... in that case...

So are you hungry? I brought home some really good pasta prima-vera, and I was waiting to eat it with you, but we don't have to eat it now. Do you just wanna sleep? Oh! And I heard the best joke today... there were these two ducks...
I'm ready.

Ready? What do you mean re...?
OH! You mean *ready*!
Uh-huh.

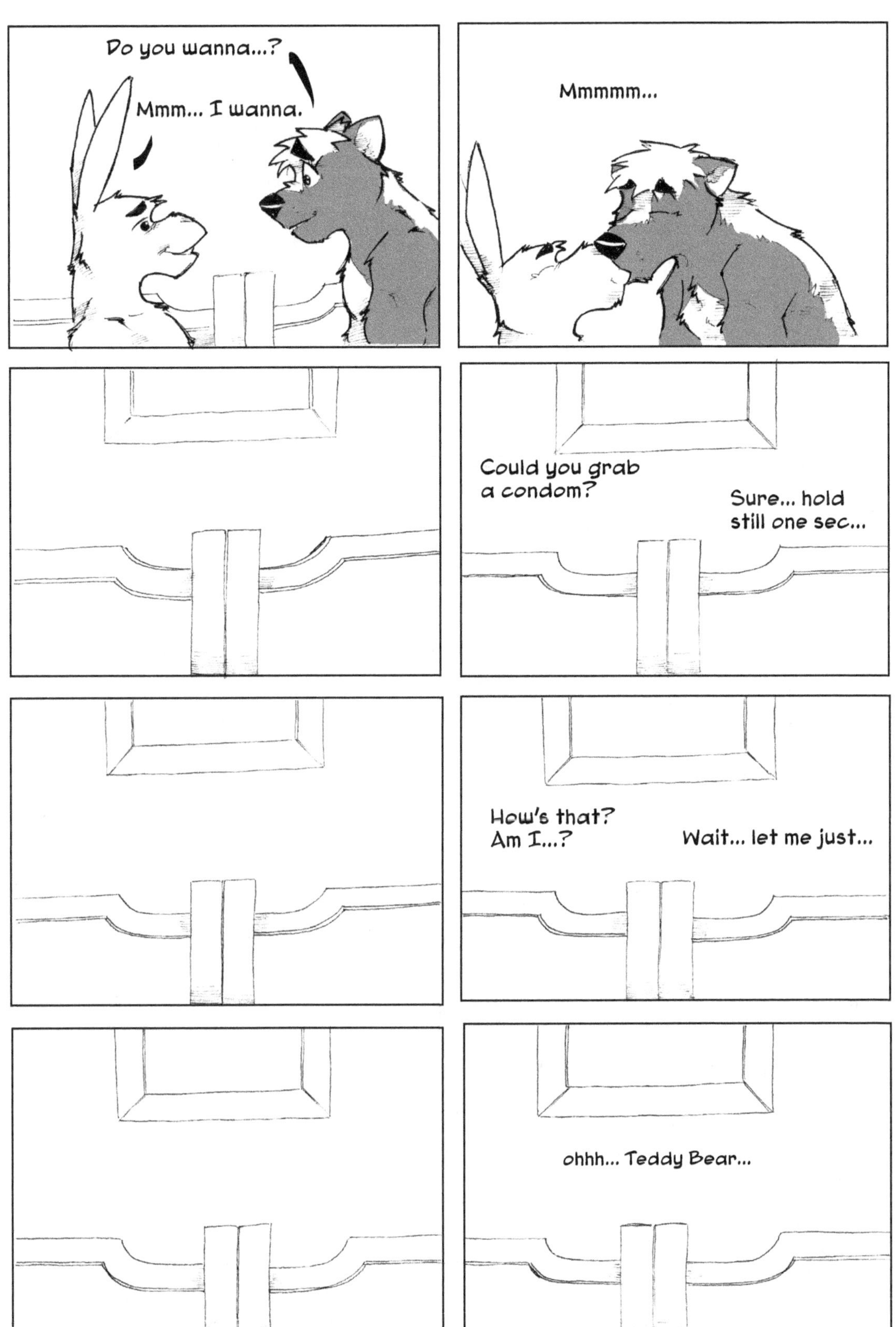
Do you wanna...?
Mmm... I wanna.
Mmmmm...
Could you grab a condom?
Sure... hold still one sec...
How's that? Am I...?
Wait... let me just...
ohhh... Teddy Bear...

*KNOCK,
KNOCK*
Coming!

Hey, Paulie. How're you?
Marty, dear, I'm so sorry to have caught you so early.
But I was wondering if we could borrow some flour. We seem to have run short.

Sure! C'mon in. I m making pancakes.
And they smell marvelous. Well, I won't keep you long.
FLOUR

Ohhhh... G'mornin', Teddy Bear! Wow... last night was completely worth waiting for! You were so...
Uhhh... Taye?

Eek! Sorry, Paulie! Didn't hear ya come in!
That's quite all right, Taye, dear. I'm not staying.

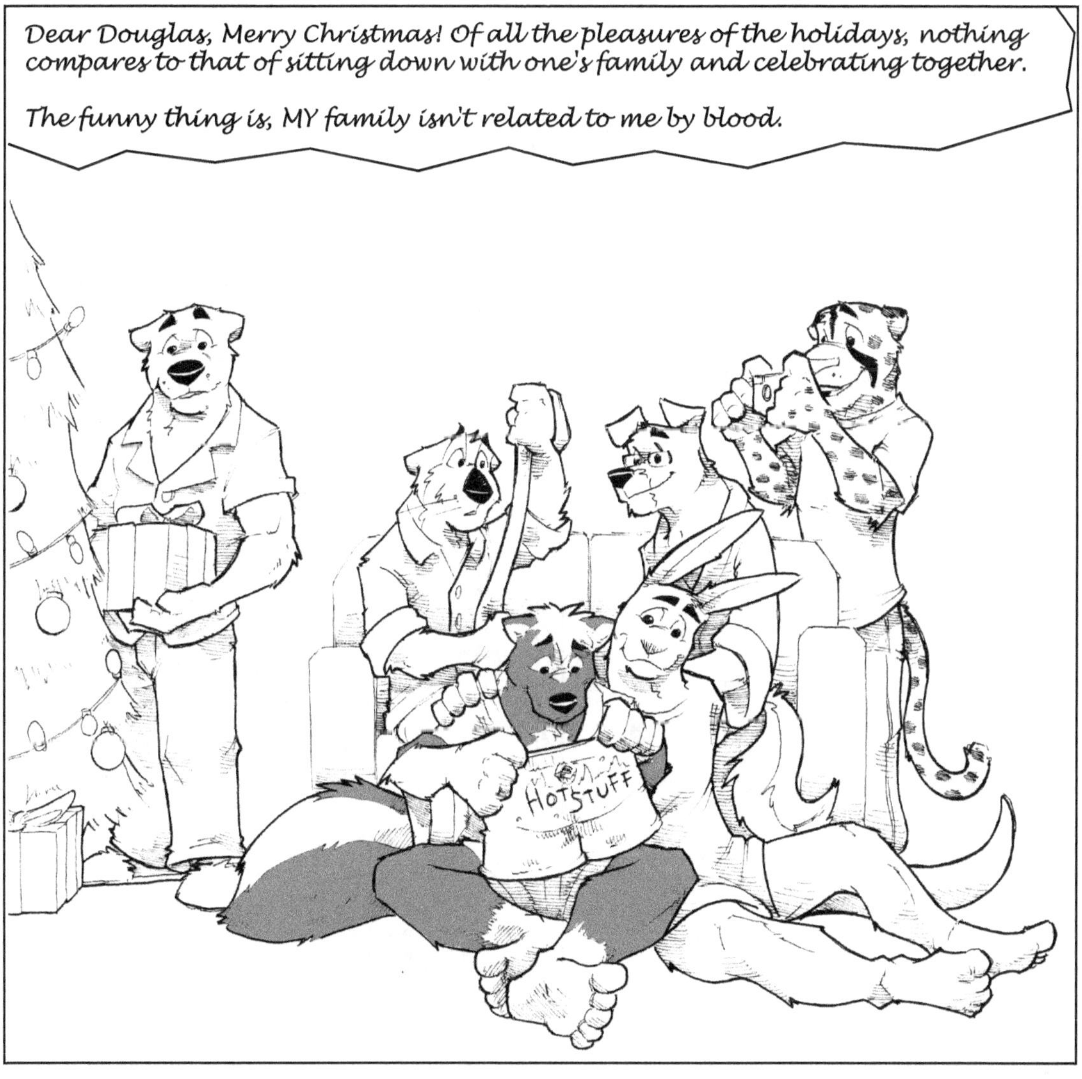

Dear Douglas, Merry Christmas! Of all the pleasures of the holidays, nothing compares to that of sitting down with one's family and celebrating together.

The funny thing is, MY family isn't related to me by blood.

I've made my family out of those I've found that I care about the most. I'm so pleased that, once a year, we have a time when we can express, in some small ways, how much we care about each other.

I'm pleased, too, that all our family's squabbles seem to be coming to an end. The world at large is hard enough on people like us without our having to make it any harder on each other.

C'mon, everyone! Family portrait! Timer's only got five seconds!

Repentant misers, virgin births, mutant reindeer... Christmas stories are full of these kinds of miracles. But, in my book, to find love and happiness in the midst of a world full of such woes... that's the true miracle.

Love, Paulie

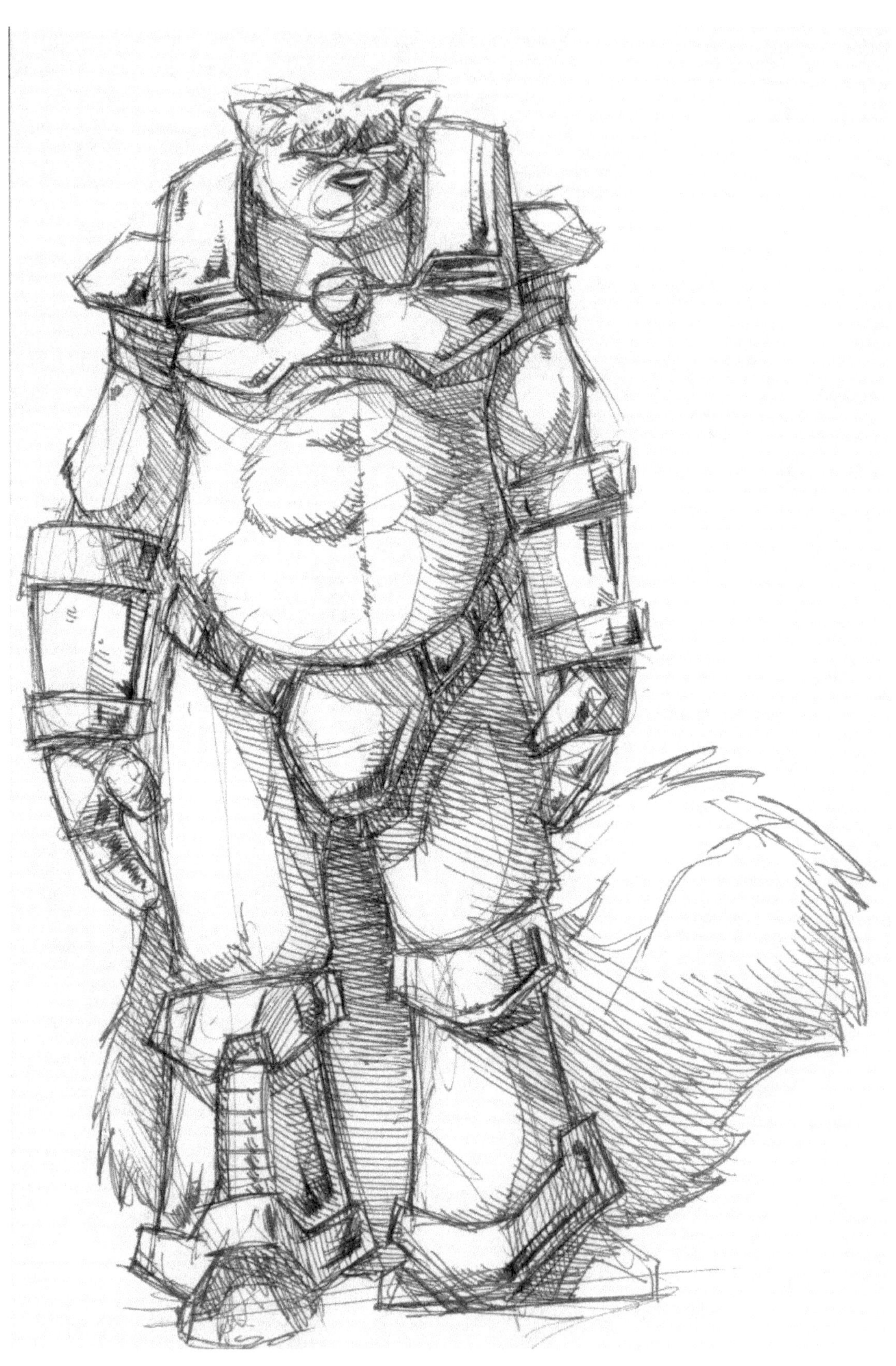

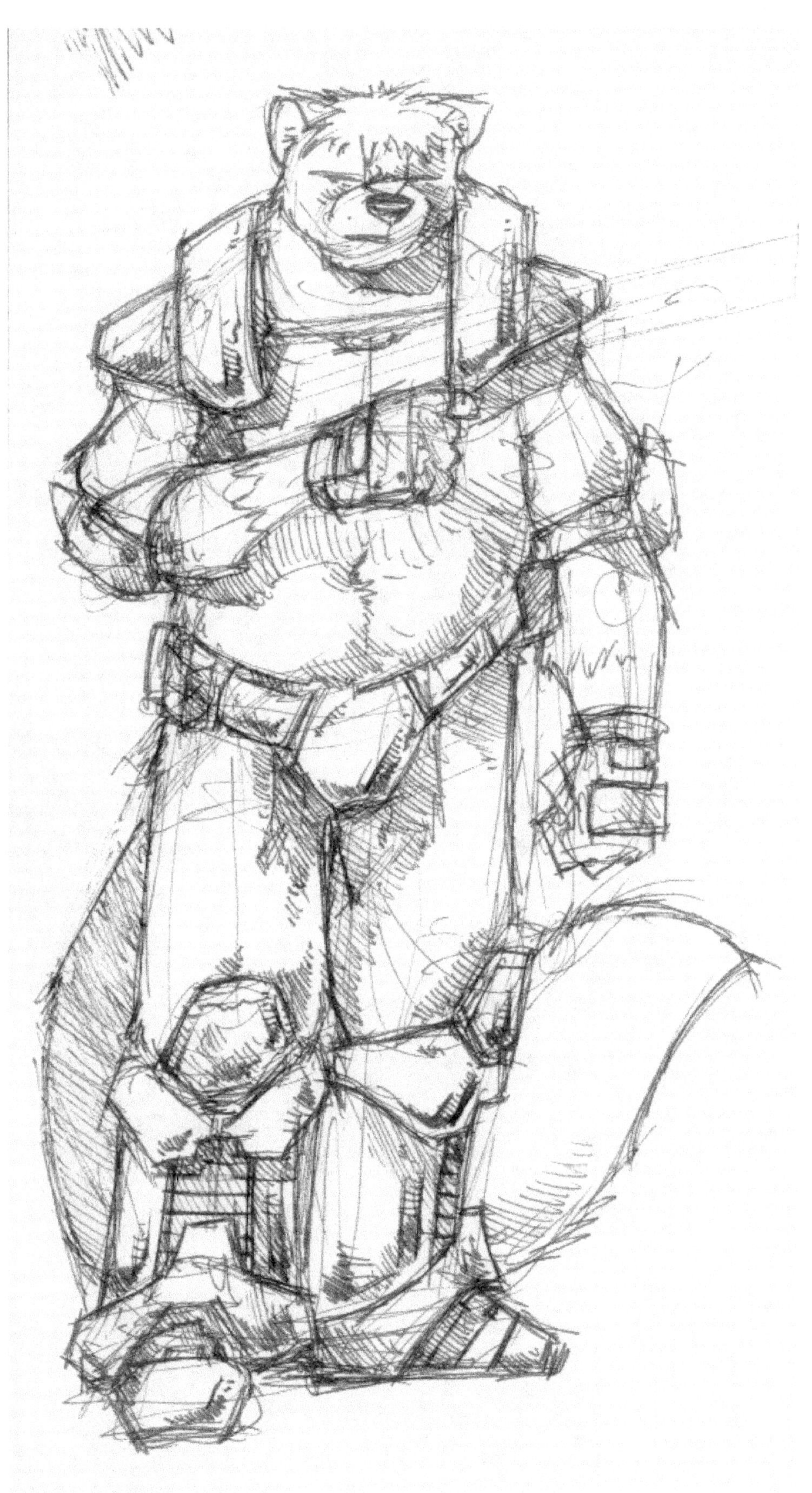

www.ingramcontent.com/pod-product-compliance
Lightning Source LLC
LaVergne TN
LVHW061245100826
845148LV00008B/1034

* 9 7 8 0 9 7 1 9 8 8 6 1 3 *